The Light Beyond the Crash

Carole Shorter

Contents

1. Chapter 1 — 1

2. Chapter 2 — 25

3. Chapter 3 — 29

4. Chapter 4 — 37

5. Chapter 5 — 43

6. Chapter 6 — 54

7. Chapter 7 — 61

8. Chapter 8 — 64

9. Chapter 9 — 76

10. Chapter 10 — 90

11. Chapter 11 — 104

12. Chapter 12 — 112

13. Chapter 13 — 117

14. Chapter 14 — 129

15. Chapter 15 — 144

16. Chapter 16 — 155

17. Chapter 17 — 162

18. Chapter 18   175

19. Chapter 19   186

20. Chapter 20   193

21. Chapter 21   206

22. Chapter 22   215

23. Epilogue   218

Chapter 1

"Wake up."

"I'm not going to tell you again, wake up." The same nightmare that she had been having again. No, this wasn't a nightmare. It couldn't be. It felt too real. And if it was just a nightmare, then she had to get herself checked. "Hello?" she called out, finally able to speak.

The voice spoke again, "Let me in."

Melanie resisted, just like she did all the time before. She looked around her, she was in her room. Or well, the nightmare was taking place inside her room. She looked over to the right of her, a desk sat on the wall, and posters of her favorite music artists sat on the wall. The lamp on her bedside table usually emitted a warm orange glow. But at this moment, it glowed a deep blue. The light from under the door gave a reddish glow. Suddenly, something started to knock on the door. The knocking got louder and louder as time went on. "Who are you?" Melanie yelled.

No response. The knocking just kept getting louder. Melanie repeated the question, louder this time. "Who are you?!"

Melanie jolted awake to her alarm, hot, sweaty, and breathing heavy. She flopped back onto her pillow "Holy shit," she whispered. "God, I hate dreaming."

"Melanie! Get your ass up, you have school in an hour." she heard her mom's voice call out from downstairs.

"Coming!" she called back.

Melanie opened her closet door and grabbed her white uniform shirt, plaid blue skirt, and a dark blue sweatshirt. She quickly changed into them just like she did every day. Once dressed, she went to the bathroom to brush her teeth. Looking in the mirror, Melanie saw how dark her under-eyes were. Even though she hated dreaming in general, she would never admit the kind of effect it had on her.

She turned on the faucet, grabbed her toothbrush, and opened her toothpaste. Just before she applied the brush to her teeth, she saw something standing behind her and whipped her head around. Nothing. Just my imagination I guess. She turned back around and got back to brushing her teeth. Though she couldn't see it, she couldn't shake the feeling that she was being watched.

Melanie spat out the minty toothpaste as she opened the door to the bathroom. She raced down the stairs and grabbed her gray backpack that was to the side of the kitchen table. Her mom handed her a banana as they walked towards the front door. The usual morning chill and the fog were there. When Melanie and her mom got on the road, her mom asked, "How did you sleep, Melanie?"

"I slept fine," a lie. "How about you?"

"I slept fine, too." her mom replied.

The rest of the car ride to school was quiet, per usual. Melanie and her family never interacted much. Even though they lived in the same house, they felt like strangers. Once they got to school, her mom dropped Melanie off on the sidewalk. "Have a good day, honey," she called before driving off.

"You too," Melanie replied.

Saint Catherine Academy, or what many referred to as "hell" was a catholic high school, the school that Melanie went to. The walls were a sickening shade of blue and white. Fluorescent lights loomed over the hallways. The school itself had a very low population, only about three hundred fifty kids. As Melanie walked the halls, the blue of the lockers started to hurt her eyes. "Mel!" a voice from behind her yelled. It was her best friend, Emory. Emory was the only person allowed to call her Mel. Melanie was also the only person allowed to call Emory 'Em'. It was their thing. "You look like you haven't slept in years."

Melanie only stared at Emory "What makes you say that" she said in a sarcastic tone.

"Uh, nevermind then." Emory laughed. "Dude Mrs. J's going to be on our asses if we aren't in class on time."

"Why?" Melanie asked.

"Uh duh, it's Thursday, remember?>" Emory responded.

"Oh shit, right we have that weekly church thing today." Melanie rolled her eyes.

"Yeah, I'm honestly just thinking of skipping." Emory said as she turned into their homeroom class with Mrs. J.

"What was that?" Mrs. J asked.

"Ugh, nothing Mrs. J." Grumbled Emory.

"That's what I thought." Mrs. J said before walking away.

"Why do we even do that here? I get that it's a catholic school but damn do they have to make it mandatory?" Emory sighed.

"Exactly, some of us are here not because we're catholic, but because we can't stand the people in public schools and want a break from it." Melanie responded, being very fluid in her hand motions.

As she spoke and moved her hand around, she felt it getting abnormally hot. Her hands were usually cold or room temperature, they were only ever hot in the summer, so it felt weird to suddenly get the feeling.

"Ow!" Melanie cut herself off as she jolted her hand close to her stomach to keep herself from moving it.

"Mel, what happened, are you okay?" Emory asked, getting out of her seat slightly to see what had happened.

"Yeah, I think I'm fine. My hand just got hot all of a sudden, it was really weird." Melanie looked up into Emory's blue eyes.

"Do you need a wet cloth, or," she paused, trying to think, "some bandages?" Emory fully sat back down in her seat.

Melanie and Emory sat at their desks and waited for the bell to ring. Once it finally did ring, the room got into a single-file line to walk over to the school's church. Saint Catherine Catholic Church, a big building with crosses that lined the walls. As soon as you walked into the doors, many would instantly get lightheaded and nauseous. The church smells heavily of weed or some other drug. Most of the students were used to the smell, as they were in there often.

But some, like Melanie and Emory, felt sick to their stomachs whenever they entered. They tried to avoid the church as much as possible. "I swear, one of these days I'm going to pass out from how bad this smell is." Melanie whined.

Emory nodded in response. "This smell is going to be the death of me."

The pews in the nave were uncomfortable. They left marks on many people's legs, some even getting rashes. As the time passed, the priest went on. His preaching seemed to go on for hours. With each passing minute, Melanie's eyes got heavier and heavier. She looked next to Emory and saw that she was asleep. Maybe just a few minutes of sleep wouldn't hurt. She thought.

When Melanie and Emory finally awoke, the mass was over. Mrs. J was standing over them. "You girls will not sleep in the mass!" she exclaimed.

Melanie and Emory looked at each other and then down to the floor. "Sorry Mrs. J." Emory said quietly.

Mrs. J walked away from the girls to line up the class to go back to the school. The first class that they had after church was physics. While walking to class, Emory grabbed Melanie's shoulder. "Girl, Mrs. J's such a bitch." she drowned out the word "bitch".

"You think?" Melanie said sarcastically.

"Do you think it's because we're gay?" Emory's eyes widened, trying to be funny.

Melanie chuckled "What?"

"Yknow, like how im BI and you're the biggest girl kisser on earth? You think she has a gaydar?" Emory chuckled to herself as the two turned into the physics classroom.

"No, I do not think that she has a gaydar. Are you high?"

"Nope, but I kind of wish that I was. My mom would kill me if I became a stoner, though."

The two of them took their seats at the table in the back. The room was painted an ugly shade of gray. Somehow it was the biggest classroom in the school, other than the gym. Ms. Lodge shuffled through a stack of papers while looking around the room, trying to see if everyone was there. "I'm going to assume that Mrs. J has not given these to you guys yet." She organized the papers as she went from her desk to the front of the classroom. "As you all should know, the sophomores, which is you all, go on a field trip to the SpeedPark theme park." She started walking around the room handing out the permission slips to the students. "I have no clue why they would choose a random year and a random date. Lucky us I guess." she groaned, sounding annoyed.

Once the permission slips made it to their table Melanie picked it up and read it. All of it was the same as their other permission slips, stuff about how the school is not liable for any damages to the students. Weird but okay. Melanie thought as she looked at Emory. Emory just shrugged. "Same bullshit that's on every permission slip." Emory rolled her eyes.

Melanie looked back down at the permission slip. "Yknow, I've been having these nightmares."

Emory looked at her "Huh? What do you mean?" she asked.

Melanie sighed. "It's just like a recurring nightmare where I wake up in my room with red and blue lights around me with a weird thing outside my door banging asking me to let it in."

Emory playfully punched Melanie "Shut up, Mel." she drowned out the "L" sound. "You know I don't like that kind of scary stuff." she laughed.

Melanie rolled her eyes, "I'm serious, Em."

"Why did you even bring it up?" Emory asked.

"I don't know, just been bothering me for a while I guess." Melanie started at the tiny half sheet of paper.

Emory just rolled her eyes as she put her slip into her bag. Melanie did the same. "How about you meet me at my house later tonight and we'll ride our bikes until sunset. Will that get your mind off of whatever 'nightmare' you're having?" Emory asked.

Melanie hesitated, yes she loved to ride bikes with Emory, but she did not think that it would take her mind off of the nightmares. "Fine." she finally responded. "Text me when I should come over."

"Great, will do." Emory cheered. The rest of the day went by fairly quickly, before Melanie knew it, Emory was already texting her to come over. Melanie looked at the message and smiled.

Come over soon, I'm almost ready :)

On my way!

Ugh, stupid autocorrect. OMWWWWWWWWW

Melanie rushed down the stairs and yelled "Bye Mom I'm going to hang out with Emory!"

"Be home before sundown, and bring your phone with you." her mom yelled back.

Melanie went to the back of her house, grabbed her bike, and walked it to the road. She got on and started riding down to Emory's house. The wind slightly messed up her blond hair, flipping it in many directions as she rode. She made her final left turn onto Emory's street. She saw Emory out in front of her house, sitting on her phone with her bike next to her. "Em!" Melanie yelled.

Emory looked up from her phone in Melanie's direction, "Hey Mel! Finally, you're here. It felt like I was waiting for hours."

"Oh shut up, it was a bit windy."

Emory got onto her bike. "Alright, alright." Emory pedaled out to the road where Melanie was.

"When is our math homework due again? She always gives us the most random due dates." Melanie asked, riding next to Emory.

"Hell if I know." Emory scoffed. "I would assume tomorrow because that's our next class with her. If I'm being honest, I'll just take a failing grade, I couldn't care less."

"That's understandable, the class is hard." Melanie said.

Riding on the streets was dangerous, especially where they lived. Many people would die in that neighborhood because of reckless drivers. You basically couldn't turn a corner without seeing a small cross with flowers by it, marking where people had died. They were all mainly children, and one or two were adults. Many "slow" signs were placed near where each person had died, trying to stop anyone else from being hit. Though, it never worked.

Melanie and Emory slowly rode down a hill. "Have you gotten your mom to sign that permission slip yet?" Emory asked.

"Have you?" Melanie replied, she had completely forgotten about it, there was still a week before they were due anyway.

"I did it right when I got home because I knew that I would forget." Emory smiled.

"I'll have to ask my mom to sign it when we're done riding." Emory sighed, "I might just forge her signature, how would anybody know?"

As they turned the last corner of their loop down to Emory's house, they were laughing. Melanie dropped Emory off at her house and started riding back to her own. On the way back, she spotted something, or, someone, in the corner of her eye. It looked like the same person that she had seen behind her in the mirror from earlier that morning. The figure was standing behind a small group of trees, just watching her. She noticed the figure's hands, inky black and pointed fingers that wrapped around the trunk of one of the trees. Melanie looked around and then looked back at the figure. It was gone, just like earlier. Melanie was now more alert and aware of her surroundings. She noticed that the roads seemed more rocky than usual. The air around her faintly smelled of rusty gasoline. After a few more minutes she eventually made it home and went inside of her house. She found her mom sitting on the couch watching the news. Melanie went to her backpack and took out her school laptop and the permission slip given to the class today. She put her laptop on a charger and went over to her mom. "Hey mom?" she asked.

"Yes?" her mom asked coldly.

"Do you mind signing this? It's for a school trip." Melanie handed over the slip to her mom.

Her mom briefly read over the contents of the slip. She then shrugged and picked up a pen that was on the coffee table. She signed it and gave it back to Melanie. "Two weeks from today, hm? And an amusement park" she asked suspiciously. She wasn't expecting her to sign it. She was ready to forge it.

Melanie took the permission slip back from her mom. "Yeah, not like anyone's going to die."

Melanie's mom nodded and went back to watching the news. Melanie went to put the permission slip back in her backpack as her mom called out to her. "Don't forget to take a shower tonight." she said, not even looking up from the couch."

"I won't." Melanie sighed and closed her backpack. She went up the stairs to get a quick shower.

While in the shower, she closed her eyes to wash her hair, holding her head under the shower head. She ran her hands through her hair to get all of the shampoo out of it. While doing so, she started to feel that the water was thicker. She couldn't tell what was wrong with it with her eyes closed. She tried to quickly open her eyes out of fear, but when she did soap got into her right eye, causing it to sting. "Fuck." she grunted as she put her hand up to her eye to cover it.

It took her a minute to open her eyes fully again without them hurting but when she did she saw blood covering her hands, face, and slowly dripping down her body. Some of it was even on the walls. She let out a loud gasp, looking down at her hands. She frantically tried to wash them in the water but the blood just kept coming. Something in her gut was telling her that this was not her blood. Tears started to well up in her eyes and she tried to rub them. When she stopped rubbing her eyes, the blood was gone. She felt her legs start wobbling and she held onto the shower handle for support.

She got out of the shower and got dressed in her night clothes. She was still shaken up from what had happened in the shower and it took her a few more minutes than usual to get changed. She grabbed her phone and texted Emory.

Emory, the craziest thing just happened.

What?

I was taking a shower and I swear to god that I was COVERED in someone else's blood.

You're delusional. I think you should think about getting professional help.

I'm serious! I'm literally shaking!

Lol, you're so delusional. Have you been sleeping?

Yes, I have! I know what I saw.

Okay well, I'm going to go eat dinner now weirdo. See you tomorrow. Try to sleep.

Ugh fine. I'm too scared to See you tomorrow.

Melanie went into her room and lay down on her bed, unable to shake what had just happened. Her room was a light purple color with fairy lights along the ceiling. Her desk was flooded with papers that she knew she had to finish for school. A few shirts were scattered on the wooden floor. She covered herself in her navy-colored bed sheets and plugged her phone into its charger. She turned on her phone and saw a message from her mom.

Food?

No thanks, not hungry.

K.

She closed her messaging app and scrolled on Instagram and YouTube for a few hours until she started to feel tired. She looked at the time at the top of the screen. It was almost one in the morning. She set her phone on her nightstand to the left of her bed and turned on some music. She hoped that if she fell asleep to it, it would help her get her mind off of what had happened earlier and maybe even stop her from having that nightmare again. Before she put her head on her pillow, she remembered that she had math homework to finish. She didn't know the due date but seeing as it was Friday, she assumed that it would be due today. Melanie groaned. Whatever, she'll just rush through it before they check it in class. She lay back down and rolled onto her right side and closed her eyes. Her playlist was faintly playing in the background. She slowly drifted off to sleep.

Melanie slowly opened her eyes, she knew she was still asleep just from the lighting. The red and blue lights seemed to engulf her room like a tsunami. She sat up in her bed, tonight's nightmare seemed too real. Melanie was more alert than she normally was. She looked over at her bedroom door. When she did, something on the other side of the door was loudly banging on it. A loud static noise started to fill her head and she covered her ears in discomfort.

"Let me in," The voice was back, speaking slowly and almost demanding.

"Let me in," it repeated, getting increasingly more demanding.

"What? Who are you?" Melanie yelled, covering her ears.

"Let me in. Let me in. Let me in." all the voice would do was get more and more demanding. It would repeat the three simple words, getting louder each time. Melanie wanted to take her eyes off of her door but she couldn't. It felt like it was calling her.

Melanie was frozen with fear and looked at the crack under the door. An inky black, bony hand slowly reached under the door, trying to unlock it. She suddenly realized that she recognized the thing's hand. It was the same hand she saw on the tree trunks while coming back from riding with Emory. "Go away!" Melanie yelled.

Melanie woke up in her bed. Her lights were off. She checked the time on her phone, it was 6:55. Five minutes before her alarm was set to go off. She also noticed that her music had stopped playing sometime when she was asleep. Melanie put her hand over her chest to check her heart rate. It was practically beating out of her chest. She turned on the fairy lights above her bed so that she could see. She looked at her bedroom door and saw nothing. She lay back down on her bed to relax herself. "What the hell?" she whispered slowly.

Melanie went downstairs to get a glass of water, fully alert and awake. The stairs quietly creaked under her feet. The sun was barely visible out of the house's side window. Melanie's mind was all over the place as she walked downstairs. What's wrong with me? Is this normal? She thought.

She flicked the light switch so that the kitchen lights turned on. Melanie opened the cupboard to grab a glass then went over to the sink. She turned the faucet on, put her cup under it, and waited for it to fill up. The water was clear running into the cup. Once Melanie felt that she had filled up the cup enough, she quickly took a sip. She kept slowly drinking her water while walking back up the stairs to get ready for school. Just one more day until the weekend. Just get through today. She thought while walking.

Melanie opened her closet, grabbed one of her uniform shirts, and pulled it off the hanger. She tossed it onto her bed and grabbed one of her skirts and her school sweatshirt off the floor. "All the same. I'll do laundry this weekend." she said holding the sweatshirt.

When she held her sweatshirt she was able to get a good look at her hands. She was shaking from the nightmare she had. She let out a deep sigh and changed into her uniform. "God, I hate this stupid school," she said as she looked at herself in the mirror.

While looking at herself, she noticed something at the side of her mouth. She stepped closer to the mirror to get a better look. It looked like a black liquid dripping down her lip. Melanie had felt it sure, but she had thought that it was just water. Seeing it made her a little sick to her stomach. She wiped it off with the back of her hand. The black liquid had acted just like water except the liquid was just a bit stickier. "The hell?" she questioned, staring at it. Melanie grabbed a tissue from her nightstand and the black stuff off of the back of her hand.

Melanie grabbed her phone again to check the time, making sure she was on time. She was, the time was 7:15. She went downstairs to check if her mom was up and ready to drive her to school. "Mom?" she called out.

A few seconds later she heard a voice come from the living room. "Mhm." her mom said, standing up from the couch. Her mom walked over to her "Come on, let's go."

Melanie nodded and took her school laptop off of its charger and into her bag. She put her backpack over her shoulder and walked with her mom to the car. The ride to school was silent, as usual. Melanie stared out of the window and then looked down at her hands, they had stopped shaking. They turned the corner onto the school's road and her mom dropped her off. "Bye, I love you." her mom said.

"I love you too, mom," Melanie responded.

Melanie's mom smiled and drove off once Melanie was out of the car. Melanie spotted Emory a few feet ahead of her walking into school. "Em!" she called out.

Emory turned around to face Melanie and waved. "Hey Mel!" she called.

Melanie quickly walked up to Emory so they could walk in together. "Did your mom sign the slip?" Emory asked.

Melanie nodded "Yeah, I doubt she even read it." she rolled her eyes.

"At least we don't have to worry about it now, right?" Emory smiled and opened the front door to walk into the school. Melanie followed behind.

"I guess you're right."

The two of them got to the classroom and sat down in their seats, it was like every morning. Everyone was always so loud and full of energy at seven in the morning.

"If you have the permission slips Ms Lodge gave to you, hand them to me." Mrs. J said, looking down at her notebook with her lesson plans.

Melanie and Emory took out their signed slips and gave them to Mrs. J. Only a few other classmates of theirs had gotten them signed. The two went back to their seats. "So Mel, did you have that 'recurring nightmare' again?" Emory said, putting air quotes around the words jokingly.

Melanie rolled her eyes, annoyed. "Yeah? What's it to you anyway? I thought it scared you."

"It did, but thinking about it, it's kind of funny."

Melanie just stared at Emory blankly. "Sure," she said, pulling on the middle of the word.

Math class was their last class, one more class until they were free for the weekend. "Alright class, pull out your home-work." Mr. Van their teacher had said.

Shit. Melanie thought. She watched as everyone else opened their laptops to their homework sheet. In turn, Melanie opened her laptop, too. She stared at the blank page and quickly tried to write in the answers. Melanie was com-pletely in the zone, not paying attention to anything other than writing in answers. She didn't even care that they were miles out of the ballpark. She finished the twelve-question worksheet in three minutes. She quickly pressed the save and turn-in buttons just as her teacher was checking to see who had turned it in. "Finally, everyone turned in their homework." their teacher had said.

Melanie let out a sigh of relief. Emory watched from the seat behind Melanie and tapped her shoulder. Melanie turned around to face Emory. "I thought you said you were going to get your homework done when you got home last night." Emory said.

"Yeah, well," Melanie paused, "I forgot." She then turned back around

Once the fifty-minute period was up, the bell rang. Melanie and Emory gathered their stuff and walked to Mrs. J's home-room. Finally, they were released to go home. Melanie and Emory walked out together to find their cars. "Are we gonna ride tonight, Mel?" Emory asked.

"You can just text me again when you want to meet." Melanie said as she waved goodbye to Emory.

"Okay, I will!" Emory smiled and gave a thumbs-up.

Melanie opened the door to her room and flopped onto her bed, digging her face into her mattress. After a few seconds, Melanie pulled out her phone and scrolled on social media for about an hour until she got a text from Emory.

Hey, come over when you're ready. I'll be waiting :)

okay, omw now

Cool

I'll be there in 5

Melanie got up quickly and started to change into more comfortable clothing. She grabbed her bike and started to ride over to Emory's house. The familiar bike ride comforted her. After a few minutes of riding, she got to Emory's house and saw her sitting on her front porch like the day before. The two of them started to ride around the neighborhood on their usual loop. "How long have we been friends again?" Emory asked.

"I think about ten years? Why?" Melanie responded.

"No reason, It just feels like it's been longer."

The two of them rode past the same group of trees that Melanie had seen the figure behind the day before. Melanie stopped pedaling and put her foot on the ground to stop her from falling over. "Wait," she said.

Emory cocked her head. "Huh? Why?"

Melanie dismounted her bike and put it down on the road verge. "Just yesterday I saw something here, behind these trees."

"Mel, I think you're insane." Emory followed Melanie.

"No I'm not!" she said as she circled the trees. She saw nothing."Maybe I am." she said as she stood firmly on the ground, whatever she had seen was not there anymore.

Emory laughed as she put her hand on Melanie's shoulder. "Admit it, you're just insane. Let's just get back to riding okay?"

Melanie nodded and the two of them picked up their bikes and continued to ride on their loop. "You pulled those math answers out of your ass didn't you." Emory said.

Melanie smiles. "Yeah, well I was too tired to do it last night."

"I thought you were too scared to sleep from whatever you said happened."

This was true, Melanie was scared to fall asleep last night, but listening to music and mindlessly scrolling on social media got her mind off of it. "In my defense, you would be scared too if you were just trying to take a shower and blood was suddenly everywhere."

"Mel, Mel, I think that was just your period." Emory laughed.

"Not when it just disappears after thirty seconds!" Melanie's voice cracked at the word 'seconds'.

"The hell?" Emory asked "I uhm," she paused, "I don't think that's normal."

"Exactly, Em! It's not!" Melanie yelled.

"Maybe you should get that checked." Emory chuckled nervously.

Melanie tried to change the subject "Have you looked at the rides at Speed Park?" Melanie asked.

"Was I supposed to?" Emory asked.

"No, but I did. I've been watching some videos of some of the ride's point of views and I'm absolutely dying to go on the roller coasters. We are going on roller coasters, right, Em?" Melanie asked.

"No shit. What's the point of going if we don't do the fun stuff? I'm not riding those lame kids rides." Emory replied. "But anything with more than two or three loops is a no for me."

"Oh, totally," Melanie said.

When she finished speaking, her bike rode over a rock, causing her to almost fall off. She was able to steady herself and didn't fall. "Oh shit, Mel. you okay?" Emory asked.

"Yeah, I'm fine. It was just a stupid rock in the road." she said as she continued to ride beside Emory.

Melanie dropped Emory off at her house like she always did and rode home. On the way back she tried not to look at the trees. When she got inside her house she saw that her mom had gone out. Melanie pulled out her phone to see if her mom had texted her about where she was going, but nothing. "Figures," Melanie grumbled.

Melanie went upstairs and sat down on her bed. She looked around her room, dirty clothes on the floor, and laundry baskets overflowing. "Gross," she said.

She sighed as she got up from her bed and turned on some music. She tried to clean her room as quickly as she possibly could. Picking up clothes off the floor was not the way she or anybody wanted to spend their Friday night. She hummed along to the songs that played on her phone. When she got all of her dirty clothes piled into two baskets, she brought them down to the basement where the washing machine and dryer were. Once she turned the washing machine on and left the basement, she went to the kitchen to look for food. She opened the stainless steel fridge, covered in her old art projects from when she was younger, random Polaroid pictures that Melanie had placed on the side of her and Emory, some of them were of her and her mom, all of her good report cards, none of the bad. Two years ago, when she was thirteen, she got an F on her report card. It was the only time that she had ever failed a class. Her mom said that if she displayed the bad report cards, people would think differently of their family. When this happened, Melanie asked "What family?" seeing as her parents were divorced, she hadn't seen her dad since the divorce, and her mom spent her days sitting on the couch watching television. She got grounded for a month after that incident.

Melanie wrapped her hand around the handle and pulled the fridge door open. She didn't see much in there other than a few apples and spoiled milk. She grabbed an apple, closed the fridge, and went back to her room. "Finally," she whispered as she leaned back to fall onto her bed.

She heard the garage door open about an hour later. Her mom came into the house but didn't say anything. Melanie didn't bother trying to say anything to her mom, either. She knew that she would just get a one-word response to anything she said. She looked at the time, it was 7:30. Melanie waited until around 8:00 to go downstairs to check again for food. She didn't eat dinner last night so she knew that she had to eat something tonight. She got up, went downstairs, and into the kitchen. She saw that her mom had made some noodles. They were pretty bland, but it was enough. "Hey, mom?" Melanie asked.

"What." her mom responded coldly.

"Can I have some of these noodles?"

"Go ahead, I already had some."

Melanie grabbed a spoon and started to scoop some noodles into a bowl. When she got enough to satisfy her, she grabbed a fork and then went back to her room. She sat on her bed, eating her food. She continued to mindlessly scroll on social media until she got a notification from her email app. She looked at the notification, the preview color of the notification seemed to be a shade darker than any other notification she had ever gotten from the app. She clicked on the notification to see what the email said.

The contents of the email were suspicious from the start of reading it. The sender didn't even have a name, it just said 'unknown sender'. Melanie decided that it wasn't important and sent it to the 'trash' file. When she closed the app, she got another notification from it. She opened the app again and read the contents of the email this time.

Blank

Unknown sender

You will let me in, whether you like it or not ;)

It is only a matter of time before you realize it.

(Attachment file 1)

X

"What the hell?" Melanie asked herself. "This has to be some kind of prank..." she said as she clicked on the attachment.

She stared at the image, confused and scared. It was a picture of her from her phone's front camera. She knew she didn't take the picture. "God damn I'm ugly at that angle." she laughed nervously.

Melanie tried to close the image but her eyes caught something about the picture before. On her forehead, there was what looked to be a drawn-on silhouette tattoo of a jackalope. Melanie quickly screenshotted the picture and the email and closed out of it, her heart beating out of her chest while she sent the screenshots to Emory.

EMORY!!!

EMORY!!! HELP!!! IT'S URGENT!!!

Huh?

(attachment: 2 images) THIS!!!

Wtf... that's super weird. Creepy much?

IDK WHAT TO DO I'M KIND OF FREAKING OUT

Just block it

Oh yeah, I can do that. THAT DOESN'T MEAN I'M NOT STILL SCARED!!!

Melanie laughed, this guy couldn't do anything. She re-opened the email and tried to block the sender. Block Unsuccessful. Melanie stared at the words, slightly shaking her head. She repetitively clicked the block button, desperate for something to work. After two or so minutes of repetitive tapping on her screen, the app closed itself. When she tried to open it back up, it wouldn't let her. "Come on," she muttered. The app eventually let her open it. The email was gone, from her inbox, the trash, spam, everything. Melanie sighed a long sigh of relief. She thought it was all over. But that couldn't be further from the truth.

The next few weeks passed by like normal. She would have the same nightmare that she had been having, wake up, go to school, and have a few weird things happen like random blood appearing on her throughout the day, but that was it. The days until the trip to Speed Park started to blend. Days passed and passed until Tuesday came, it was two days before the trip. Melanie got up for school and saw bruises on her arms. They looked like lines crawling up her forearms and into her shoulders. "Oh my god, what happened to me? They weren't here last night." Melanie asked herself. She tried to touch one of them, but it made her wince in pain. Melanie decided to just cover them with her sweatshirt and went to school.

Chapter 2

History was Melanie's worst subject. The only reason that she was passing the class was because she turned in all of her homework. She fails every test and quiz no matter how hard she tries. Her seat was in the back of the class by the window. She stared out of it, thinking about all of the weird things that had been happening. What is happening to me? The nightmares I can deal with but the blood and emails and shit? There is no way I'm going to deal with that. Her mind continued to swim in thoughts until her teacher's voice spoke. "I expected better from you Ms. Adelia," he said, setting a recent test on her desk. A 'F' sat in the corner of the front page. Melanie stared at the paper for a few seconds before slowly putting it into her desk to throw away later. She looked up and over to Emory who was across the room from her. Emory looked happy, she always did well on these tests.

After class, Emory came up to Melanie and spoke, "Hey how'd you do on the test?" Emory smiled.

"What do you think?" Melanie asked sarcastically.

"I'm guessing terrible."

"Yeah! None of it made any sense! Did we ever even learn about the seventeenth amendment?" Melanie banged her books on her forehead.

"We went over it for four days straight."

"Well, I wasn't there then!" Melanie protested.

"You have to be joking. You haven't missed a day of school since second grade."

Melanie knew that it was true, she hated having absences on her attendance record. "Then explain how I still failed."

"It's confusing, don't worry about it. Hey, at least you're passing right?" Emory asked, walking down the hallway.

"Yeah, I think so. I'll have to check my grades because I'm pretty sure that that test brought it down a lot." emphasizes the word 'A lot'. Melanie and Emory walked into the physics classroom and sat down at their table.

Melanie pulled out her laptop and logged into their school's grading system. She elbowed Emory until she looked over to her. "How low do you think these are going to be?" she smirked.

"Imagine if you're failing every class." Emory responded jokingly.

"Oh haha, you are so funny." Melanie's voice was filled with sarcasm as she typed in her password.

The website's homepage was boring and ugly to look at. The ugly shade of blue and dirty yellow slightly burned her eyes. She clicked on the 'my grades' tab to check how terrible she knew they would be. "How in the hell?" she asked herself.

"What is it? Are they that bad?" Emory turned her head to her friend.

"How the fuck do I have straight A's?"

Emory's eyes widened. "What? How? You're joking, right? You have to be joking."

"See for yourself." Melanie turned her laptop to face Emory.

"Holy shit, good job."

"This has to be a joke, even in history I have an A." "Be happy, Mel!" Emory started as she put a hand on Melanie's shoulder. "With our grading scale, even one or two A's is really good!"

The grading scale fucking sucked. Everyone knew it, even the teachers. Anything under seventy-five percent was a failing grade. That mixed with the shitty teachers, so many kids over the years had failed a bunch of classes. "Well if I've been failing every single history test, I don't think that I would have an A in the class." Melanie shut her laptop and looked over to Ms. Lodge who was at her desk, waiting for the bell to ring to start the class.

When the bell rang, Ms. Lodge started talking "Are you guys excited for your trip on Thursday?" she asked.

The class erupted in excited cheers. "How long's the bus ride?" a boy in the front of the class asked.

"If I remember correctly, it's about an hour and a half ride."

Most of the class groaned, not happy about how long the ride will be. "What happens if we crash?" a chatty red-haired girl asked.

That's such a stupid question. Melanie thought there's no way that we're going to crash. The drivers know how to drive, at least they should know, and it won't be crowded with a lot of traffic because it's a weekday.

"Well, let's just hope that doesn't happen."

"And if it does?" the redhead continued to question.

"If it does, hopefully, it won't be that bad and cause anybody to die."

Chapter 3

Melanie sat in her room, it was late. Far too late to be up on a school night. Something wouldn't let her fall asleep. She kept tossing and turning all night even with her eyes closed but nothing helped. She pulled her body up so that she was sitting up in her bed and stared at the wall and into the mirror on the wall. Studying her reflection in the dark. Her body was barely outlined in her already dark room. While looking at herself, she saw something in the mirror behind her. The same shadow figure wrapped its hands around Melanie in the reflection of the mirror. Its hands looked like claws, holding her in place. Its claws were large and dark like the night sky. She couldn't scream, she couldn't do anything at all. She was just frozen in place. She couldn't even look away. She could feel the creature's hands wrap around her shoulders, pulling on her. Its hands pulled so tight it felt like it was digging into her skin, trying to pull out her bones. She couldn't feel anything, but she could see it. From behind her in the reflection, she could see a dark shadow-like head slowly come up. Its piercing eyes stared into hers from the reflection. Melanie jumped forward, using all of her strength to look away from the mirror as well by closing her eyes. When she opened them, she quickly turned on her fairy lights to illuminate the room. She grabbed a blanket and put it over the mirror. She lay back down in her bed, lights still on. The familiar feeling of tiredness finally swept over her. She shut her eyes tight and wrapped her blanket around her for comfort. Eventually, she was able to fall asleep.

The next morning she woke up and saw the blanket that she had placed over her mirror had fallen. At school, she could barely focus from the lack of sleep. The classes were blending together as she was falling asleep in most of them. Throughout the entire day, Emory was looking at Melanie with a concerned look but didn't ask any questions. "Hey Em, are we going to ride around the neighborhood later tonight?" Melanie asked.

"We can if you want, but you for one look super tired and our trip is tomorrow so we may want to get a lot of sleep if we're planning on walking around a lot. Speaking of sleeping, did you get any of it last night? You legit look possessed or... undead or something."

"That's true, about the walking part. But you try sleeping when you keep seeing shadow creatures and having the same goddamn nightmare every night where some literal creep whose face I can't even see begs for me to let it in." Melanie grumbled.

"I'll take that as a no then." Emory sighed.

"Mhm. Well, I guess then I'll see you tomorrow," she spoke with a lot of air in her words as she walked away.

At home, Melanie put the fallen blanket over the mirror again while sighing. Why the hell was this all happening to her? Was she going insane? She lay down on her bed and scrolled on Instagram for a few hours until she got an email. She opened it, curious.

Blank

Unknown Sender

You naive little girl, I believe we both know that a little blanket won't stop me :)

X

Melanie's eyes widened in fear. I thought I had blocked this bitch. She thought to herself. This time, there was no image but it still scared her shitless. Melanie tried to block whoever was sending these emails but she just got the same message that she got a few weeks ago: Block Unsuccessful. Melanie knew that it would be better to just delete the email and try to forget about it until she figured out how to do something about it but she wanted to reply to it so bad, playing into whoever's game this was. Melanie started a reply:

Re: Blank

Melanie.Adelia @ gmail.com

This isn't funny y'know... Whoever the hell you are...

Melanie quickly deleted all of it, knowing that it was a bad idea. She quickly trashed the email and went back to scrolling on Instagram. A few hours later, the sun had gone down and it was pitch black out. Melanie thought for a moment about what Emory had said earlier that day at school; Our trip is tomorrow so we may want to get a lot of sleep if we're planning on walking around a lot.

She quietly laughed to herself, "Heh, what does she know? I'll be fine." she slightly smiled.

A few more hours passed, quicker than Melanie expected. She looked over to her mirror to check if the blanket was still covering it, it was. Melanie started to feel her eyes getting heavy. She kept her eyes open to try and fight sleep, still scrolling on Instagram. After ten-ish minutes of fighting it, she finally fell asleep.

Red and blue lights surrounded her again, she was dreaming. They usually blended together nicely, but now one eye saw red, and the other saw blue. This time, she could feel the ground beneath her feet or more like her body. She was lying face down on her bedroom floor. She couldn't speak either, all she could do was think. What the hell? She thought. Suddenly, she heard something. The same deep voice from her nightmares before began to speak. "I told you that that blanket over the mirror wouldn't stop me."

She felt one of its hands wrap around her right shoulder. Melanie tried to move but still couldn't. A cold object pressed at the top of her back, she could tell that it was sharp from a slight cut into her spine. She felt a stabbing pain at the top of her spine as if a knife was slowly stuck into her. Melanie could feel her body freeze and tense up. This is just a dream, I'll wake up soon. I have to. This isn't real, god dammit just wake up. She tried to reason with herself, she knew that all of this had to just be a dream, right? The stabbing pain at the top of her spine slowly made its way down to her lower back, there was no way that whatever this thing was wasn't cutting into her with a knife. She silently screamed from the pain.

She could feel blood pooling out of her back and onto the wooden floor under her. Her flesh being ripped apart down the middle made her sick to her stomach. Even though she was on the ground, her legs started to feel weak from the pain. Once she felt the blade come out of her back, she could practically hear her heartbeat. It was beating loud as fast, pure fear took over her body. She then felt a cold hand reach into the exposed flesh on her back, pulling out her spine with a loud and wet crack and then grabbing onto the bones in her ribcage, pulling them out of her body, two at a time. Twelve times she felt the pain of hands pulling out her bones. Every time it hurt more and more as it went down. Each bone took more time getting out depending on how much lung tissue was in its way. Whatever this creature was was ripping up her lungs while pulling out her ribs. Melanie was unable to breathe because of the amount of damage done to her lungs. She slowly felt her vision fading out, losing contact with reality. The pain was too much for her and she could feel her eyes starting to shut. She would fade in and out of consciousness as she started to see the blood that had been pooling around her since all of this started. The creature just laughed as it continued, its deep tone suggested that it was all very far from over. She continued to fight the urge to pass out but it took over and her vision went dark.

She opened her eyes again to see morning sunlight making its way through her curtains. She was drenched in sweat and her entire body ached. Her breathing was very rapid. She sat up and wrapped her arms around her knees. Looking over to the mirror, she saw that the blanket had fallen off of it again. She sighed heavily then put her hands behind her neck, slightly shutting her eyes, calming herself. She grabbed her phone and looked at the time, seven AM. Melanie slowly got up out of her bed, cautiously setting her foot on the floor. She went over to the mirror, grabbed the blanket, and set it on her bed. "I'm done with this shit," she grumbled to herself as she started to get changed.

Because of their trip that day, they were allowed to wear any shirt with their school's logo and any shorts that they wanted to wear. Melanie put on an old shirt from freshman year that said "Saint Catherine XC". Last year, she tried out cross country with Emory and that did not go the way that they had planned. Both Melanie and Emory hated going to the practices, especially when it was hot. The races also sucked. Neither of them ever drank water while they were on the team which made them very unwell while they would practice. Emory once fell during one of the races and scraped her knees and hands badly. Neither of them had run since. Melanie laughed at the memory then she remembered people saying that they would be back later than the time that they normally get dismissed so she grabbed her charger and a power bank. She hated being in an unfamiliar place when she had a dead phone. Setting all of her things into her bag and putting it over her shoulder made her suddenly get a sinking feeling in her stomach. She swallowed it and left her room. While she walked down the stairs, she heard her mom call to her. "What time do you get back?"

Melanie started to think, trying to remember what time her classmates and teachers had said they would be back. "Four PM I think."

"Okay, not too long after your normal dismissal time." her mom started to

"I'm just happy we get to miss weekly mass." Melanie grumbled as her mom unlocked the door.

Her mom sighed while unlocking the car and getting in. When they got to the school, Melanie got out of the car and waved goodbye to her mom. "Stay safe today, okay?" her mom said.

"I will, don't worry about me." Melanie smiled as she closed the door and walked away into the school building. When she walked into Mrs. J's classroom, she saw Emory sitting at their table. Melanie went and sat down next to her. Melanie noticed that Emory looked tired. "Dang, you're the one who looks terrible today. What happened to getting a lot of sleep?" Melanie asked.

"Mel, Mel, I swear to god you telling me about your nightmares made me have them too."

Melanie sat there in shock. "What? I told you about those like two weeks ago."

"You brought it up yesterday though!"

"That is true, but I don't think that I talked about it that much. So what happened in it?"

"Yes you did, you went into detail! And whatever you said was happening to you. The knocking on the door. The weird lights and everything." Emory pulled her arm down her face, starting from her forehead and ending at the crook of her neck.

"At least you'll be able to sleep on the bus, right?" Melanie put her hand on Emory's shoulder.

"That's only if our class shuts the fuck up for once." Emory rolled her eyes. "We're allowed to have our phones on the bus too, right?"

"Yeah, that's what the teachers said."

"Thank god. I am not going an hour on a bus with these dumbasses without my phone."

Melanie chuckled as Mrs. J started to speak. "Alright class, line up now. The bus is waiting for you outside."

Their entire class quickly lined up, leaving Melanie and Emory in the back of the line. As the two tenth-grade home-room classes walked out of the school and over to where the bus was, Emory asked, "We're gonna sit in the front of the bus, right?"

Melanie looked at her "Oh hell yeah. There is no way that we will be in the back of the bus with these rampaging kids."

"Oh thank god. Yeah, no way we're going to deal with that."

Chapter 4

The bus was the normal school bus that they used to get people to school and back home. The white interior mixed with the dark blue leather seats was familiar to everyone. The bus smelled like a weird mix of cleaner and baby oil. Melanie and Emory were the last people to get on the bus. Even the teachers had gotten on before them. Luckily, the only seat open was the very front seat. As Melanie turned into the seat behind Emory, she noticed the red-haired girl who asked about the bus crashing sitting a few rows behind them. Melanie felt her stomach sink to the ground as she sat down next to Emory. Emory had the window seat, and Melanie sat next to the aisle. She put her hands together and looked around the bus with her eyes, studying it. She looked for a way out if there was an emergency. It clearly showed in her body language. "Emory, what happens if we crash?"

"C'mon, you seriously don't think that that's going to happen right?" Emory slightly raised her eyebrow to the question.

"No... well maybe a little bit. It's just what that girl said in class. Fuck what was her name?"

"Beats me. But you shouldn't get so worked up over something that isn't likely to even happen." Emory said, trying to comfort Melanie.

"You're right, you're right. It won't happen. The driver knows how to drive, right?"

"He looks like he knows how to drive." Emory said, motioning over to the bus driver who was across from them on the other side of the bus.

Melanie looked over to the driver, he was a bald man who looked to be in his fifties. His head was slightly drooping at the wheel. "He looks higher than a kite!"

"Oh shut up he does not." Emory playfully slapped Melanie's arm.

"Hey, I'm just saying what I see. And I see that he looks higher than a kite!" Melanie protested.

As the bus door closed, Melanie and Emory noticed that everyone else in their class was on their phones, still talking to each other and taking pictures. Emory took out her phone and started to play some games on it. "Oh my god, the cell service is going to suck on the bus." Emory groaned.

"It's going to be even worse in that part surrounded by that weird forest."

"Oh yeah, I forgot that that's on the drive there. Didn't they find a body in that forest recently?" Emory tried to recall the news article that she had read recently.

"They did?" Melanie asked, surprised.

"Pretty sure. It was found pretty deep into the forest too. Some people think it was a suicide but the autopsy report hasn't come out yet." Emory continued.

"Holy shit that's insane."

"Yeah, and I'll show you the article if I can find it again."

Melanie nodded as the bus started to drive off of the school's campus. Melanie pulled out her phone and put on her headphones. She turned on her music and sat with the upper part of her back on the seat, slightly slouching. She then turned to Emory. "I thought you said that you were going to try to sleep on the way over there."

"Yeah well, I also said that I would only sleep if our class shut the fuck up for once." Emory chuckled as she continued to play games on her phone.

Melanie rolled her eyes and zoned into her music. The bus had a lot of windows, especially around the front where they were. Melanie could see the road in front of the bus that they were driving on. She could see every turn that they were going to make before they made it. It comforted her, having some sense of what would happen next. It also helped her get her mind off of the thought of a possible bus crash. Melanie let out a loud sigh as she closed her eyes for a few moments. She knew that it would be another forty-five minutes until they got close enough to the park for anyone to be excited. When she opened her eyes again, it was because Emory was tapping on her shoulder. "Mel, Mel, wake up. I think they're about to start a fight!" Emory said eagerly.

Melanie looked over down the aisle to see two of her classmates arguing. She remembered one of them being more of the violent type. He was quick to anger and would fight over anything. Another one of the students Melanie recognized as Megan. "Holy shit is that Megan? Why is she arguing with some random boy?"

"Megan? Oh my god, that is Megan." Emory gasped.

Megan used to be friends with Melanie and Emory; the three of them had known each other since second grade. Then in seventh, a new girl, Brittany, came to their school. Megan wanted to be nice so she became friends with Brittany. She slowly drifted away from Melanie and Emory. Brittany started to bully their classmates, dragging Megan along with her. Melanie and Emory felt betrayed, to say the least, but got over it about two years ago. Both Brittany and Megan were somehow sent to the same high school that Melanie and Emory were sent to. It annoyed them but they knew that if they stayed out of their way that it would be fine. And that's what they did, Brittany and Megan didn't say even a word to them in the two years that they have been here. On the bus, Brittany and Megan sat at the start of the back of the bus, where every other "popular" or "cool" kid sat. Melanie couldn't hear what they were arguing about over her music blasting in her headphones. Can they just shut up already? She thought to herself.

"The only reason you're 'popular' is because of Brittany being social enough to talk to people." the boy said to Megan.

"Oh shut up, Matthew. You're just mad that Brittany rejected you last year." Megan replied.

"What? No! Shut up!" Matthew protested as he sat back down in his seat.

The rest of the back started laughing as Matthew's face turned beet red. They all seemed to be having more fun than they would at Speed Park. The bus driver, on the other hand, looked annoyed and tired of hearing students yelling and laughing. Melanie sunk back into her seat, Forty more minutes then we hopefully can get away from these demons."

Emory nodded "Oh my god. The fight was interesting but it didn't get physical. Lame in my opinion."

"You're terrified of gore and blood and shit but love physical fights?" Melanie questioned.

"So? Can those things not go together?" Emory smiled.

Melanie sighed. "You said earlier that there was a forest on our way over to SpeedPark? You said they found a body in there."

"Oh yeah, I did. I'm pretty sure it's coming up in a few minutes. Oh here look, I found the article." Emory handed her phone over to Melanie.

"Local North Carolina resident found dead in the woods on Interstate forty. Locals believe that the man committed suicide but first responders believe that it was a murder." she read out. "Hm, that's really weird. Have there been any other deaths in that forest?" She handed the phone back to Emory.

"I think that's the only one. They found him super close to the road too, it sucks that the guy was so young." Emory sighed.

Melanie nodded and looked out of the front window of the bus, watching every gradual turn. A few minutes into this, she started to notice the bus swerving. Slowly from side to side, then more and more as the minutes passed. Melanie looked over at the bus driver, his head was drooping and a shadow was cast on the man's shoulders and head. Melanie tapped

Emory "Em, look at the driver. I think we're going to die." she pointed to the bus driver.

Emory chuckled nervously "Oh my god, I think we're fucked."

"You think?" Melanie asked sarcastically.

As the bus continued to drive, trees started to surround the road. The guide rails stopped as they entered the forest. "Dude didn't somebody die in this forest?" a few kids whispered.

Some kids replied with annoyance, the others replied with a few scared whimpers. Melanie could feel her stomach sink as the bus started to swerve more. The driver's head seemed to be being pushed down by something that nobody on the bus could see. As they got deeper into the forest, the swerving just continued to get worse and worse. They were all lucky that the road for one; wasn't too busy, and two; it was a one-way freeway. Then, the bus stopped swerving. It stayed going straight for about thirty seconds, with no swerves, just a straight path. Melanie could feel her muscles immediately stop tensing. Melanie felt Emory's hand on her shoulder. "Stop stressing, Mel. It's fine now-" Emory got cut off as everyone on the bus started to scream. Melanie looked out the front window and saw that the driver had started swerving again. This time, it immediately went into a ditch, then engine first into a tree.

Chapter 5

A loud bang noise rang out, vibrating around the metal interior of the bus. Glass on most of the windows were shattered instantly. Melanie remembered closing her eyes as the bus went into the ditch. Her body jolted slightly when they hit the tree. When she opened her eyes she looked around at her body, no broken bones, no blood, not even a tiny bruise on her body. She looked over to Emory, she was just sitting there, hands out in front of her, she was shaking, and so was Melanie. "What the fuck just happened?" Emory asked with a shaking voice.

Melanie looked around to her classmates and teachers on the bus "I don't know." her voice trailed off as she saw that everyone else on the bus had passed out with just a few visible scrapes on people's arms and heads.

"Mel, we need to get help! We're the only people who are conscious and can call someone." The bus driver looked to have gotten the worst of it, a few branches had come through the window and punctured his body.

Melanie looked out of the broken window next to Emory. The beautiful green of the trees and the warm North Carolina air mixed with the smoke coming from the engine was broken by a small purple light in the distance. Something about it made Melanie drawn to it. "Wait." Melanie trailed off as she slowly tried to stand up. "Grab your stuff. Can you stand?" Melanie held onto the seat as she stood up. She felt no pain anywhere in her body. She grabbed her bag and put it over her shoulder.

Emory grabbed her bag and did the same as Melanie to stand. "Yeah, why? We need to get help. I can try to call somebody, but I'm not too sure how good the service will be since we're all the way out... here." She gestured to the forest around them.

"I think you should be more worried about how we're not dead. We were in front of this thing."

"We have to call the police! Or an ambulance! Or... something!"

Melanie went over to the bus door, noticing that it was slightly wedged open. Taking advantage of this, she grabbed one side of the door as Emory watched. She pulled the door open, just enough for her and Emory to squeeze their way out of the bus. "Em, come with me." Melanie flapped her hand back and forth quickly to get Emory to come with her.

Emory went over to Melanie as Melanie slipped through the door and out of the bus, into the forest they were in. "I'm calling an ambulance." Emory was starting to breathe heavily as she pulled out her phone with shaky hands.

"Hold on Em," she started and held a hand out in front of Emory, "do you see that light up ahead?" she pointed to the purple light she saw in the bus.

"Yeah, but I don't see what that could possibly have to do with the LITERAL BUS CRASH THAT WE WERE JUST IN!" Emory screamed.

"If there's light, there's probably a person over there. It's the quickest way to get help." Melanie started walking towards the purple light.

"And what if there isn't anybody over there? What do we do then?" Emory asked as she stood there and watched Melanie walk to the light.

"Then we can call for help. Just come on, I have a feeling that we're here for a reason." Melanie kept walking with her eyes fixed on the light ahead of her. Its purple glow was nothing short of beautiful. It glowed through the trees, almost like a beacon, telling Melanie to follow it.

Emory finally went against her better judgment, put her phone away, and followed Melanie. The two of them followed the light until it got brighter, showing them that they were getting closer to whatever the source of the light was. The two of them hopped over branches, almost running towards the light. Twigs snapped underneath their feet as they walked. As they neared the light, they noticed a building. It was old and rusted with some parts of the building looking like it was about to fall off. The light was coming from inside of the building, showing through broken windows. There was vegetation growing all over the building. "Holy shit," Melanie whispered breathly. "Come on, let's go inside. There has to be someone in here!"

"Woah, woah, woah, Mel, you're joking right? There's no way on God's green earth that I'm going in there." Emory took a step backward, away from the building.

Melanie went and grabbed Emory's wrist, pulling her to the building. Melanie pushed the metal doors of the building open. When she pushed, there was a bit of resistance from the building's age. "Come on, it can't be that bad. We'll be out of here in a minute."

Melanie let go of Emory as the building's door closed. She pulled out her phone and turned on its flashlight. "What is this place?" Melanie asked softly to the air.

"It looks like some sort of old warehouse," Emory started as she pulled out her phone and turned on its flashlight as well. "Probably built in the seventies and abandoned in the nineties."

As the two of them kept walking to where the purple light was coming from, they noticed glass doors keeping the light contained. Looking around the hall, there was broken glass, cockroaches and ants, rusty metal pipes, and random vegetation in the tile cracks all over the floor. Melanie put her hand around the handle and pulled the glass door open to get to whatever was causing the light. The room itself couldn't have been bigger than an average family room. The light that they saw was coming from two small lights connected to the wall. Above the lights, there was a big monitor screen and a few smaller ones on the sides of it. Under the big one, there was a small table that displayed two hollow, circular objects. They were too far away for either Melanie or Emory to be able to tell what they were. All of the screens were turned off, and even though the building was abandoned twenty years before they were born, all of the monitor screens looked fairly new. When Melanie shut the door, the lights under the screen started to flicker and the big monitor in the center of the room began to display static. Melanie looked at Emory. "There has to be someone here, right? There's no other way that this building can be getting power."

"I think it may be some sort of generator?" Emory replied.

"If it is a generator, then how is it on if the place is abandoned?" Melanie said as she moved her flashlight around the room. She walked over to the monitor and looked around for any wires. "It's completely wireless."

"Okay, can we call the ambulance now? I think you've forgotten that our whole grade is probably dying on a bus that could probably catch on fire at any moment! And we are just standing here in this god-forsaken warehouse that has some creepy shit going on in it." Emory ranted on and on as Melanie tried to drown her out.

"Would you shut up? Don't call an ambulance just yet," she said, annoyed as she fidgeted with the back of the big monitor.

Emory started to pace back and forth in the room, wall to wall. "No, I will not shut up! We have to call someone! And what the hell are you doing?"

"I'm finding a way to get this thing on."

"It's probably old as hell if this place is abandoned! Why even bother?" the panic in Emory's voice slightly concerned Melanie.

"Look at the model on this, it's from the 2010's. That means it's not as old as this warehouse. I'm more confused on how there was this much vegetation and cracks if it's been abandoned for just over ten years. It's not possible."

"Unless it's some weird weathering thing. How do you even know any of this?" Emory started to dial 9-1-1 on her phone.

"I have a lot of free time." Melanie stepped back from the screen as it turned on, glowing a bright neon purple.

Emory slowly put her phone down. "Wait what? If you can do this, do you know something about the bus or how it crashed?"

"Probably just a tired driver or something. Maybe even 'magical spirits from the other side' making him go off course." Melanie put air quotes around her words.

"Oh shut up." Emory rolled her eyes.

Then, around the room, a deep laughter rang out, slowly fading away until it went completely silent. "What was that?" Emory asked, almost dropping her phone.

"I..." Melanie trailed off as she faced Emory "...I don't know." Melanie then took a step to the side and put her hand on the left wall. Melanie then realized something, the laugh sounded familiar.

Too familiar.

The screen suddenly flashed a blinding indigo color, lighting up the entire room. Melanie and Emory closed their eyes and covered their faces with their arms. When the screen finally dimmed, there was a picture shown on it. Surrounded by purple-tinted static, a black silhouette of a shadowy man with a Jackalope mask stared them down as it opened its eyes. Its eyes were the same color as the screen that flashed a few seconds ago. "What the fuck is going on, I have to get help. This," Emory gestured around the room, "is too weird."

"No need," a deep voice started, "I have already called an ambulance for your little bus situation out there." Melanie and Emory turned to the monitor and saw the thing on the screen's 'mouth' move.

"See Em, I told you we'd find help here." Melanie froze as something in her suddenly clicked. The voice of the shadow man on the screen was the same one that she had been hearing in her dreams. She took a step back when she realized.

"I am much more than help, my dear. I am more of a savior." The creature smiled, "I believe we have met before, Melanie, was it?"

Melanie narrowed her eyes. "You're the one from my dreams aren't you?"

"Correct!" the man said eagerly.

Emory turned her head to face Melanie and mouthed what the fuck? To her.

"And you must be Emory," he smiled. "I was in your dream just last night as well."

"You didn't tell me you had a dream about this guy too," Melanie whispered to Emory.

"Well you just said that you heard a deep voice so I thought it was just a generic deep voice." Emory responded.

Melanie looked at the man on the screen. "Well, I think we should be going back to the bus so we don't have to explain what we're doing to the paramedics when they get here," Melanie stuttered through her words, "nice meeting you though." she wanted to get out of there, and fast. Why did she even go in there in the first place?

As Melanie went to open the door she heard it lock. How the hell? She thought.

"Now, girls. Stay for a moment, it will be a while until they get here." he continued to smile through the screen.

Melanie and Emory felt their bodies being pulled closer to the screen as the man chuckled once again. "My name is Xeno and like I said before, I can be a savior to the two of you but only if you let me in."

"Let you in where?' Emory questioned.

"Well, your mind of course!" Xeno let out a deep chuckle. "I promise that I will keep the process as slow and painless as possible for the two of you."

Melanie chuckled nervously, "I don't think we need a savior, though."

"I can help you in more ways than just one, Melanie. Something I don't think you understand is that I can see the future. And without me," He paused, "you'll be dead in a month. I'll be like a friend to you two, just a friend who's in your mind."

"If we agree, can we leave?" Melanie asked.

Xeno's eyes widened "Of course. There will be some things that I must go over first."

Melanie looked to Emory and the two nodded slowly together. "Fine, what is it?"

"See, I knew you would agree. All you will have to do is do anything that I say without any questions, got it?"

"And what kind of things will you have us do? Nothing weird right?" Melanie asked.

"Mel!" Emory exclaimed.

"What? These are valid questions!"

"And in the time you're asking these questions, we could've been out of here!"

"Relax, relax," Xeno cut in, "and no it won't be anything weird."

"Okay, then can we get to it? I really really don't want to have to answer any questions about this place." Emory grumbled.

Xeno laughed, "Alright, then, there are two bracelets on the table under me. Grab them and put them on."

Melanie and Emory walked over to the table and saw two indigo bracelets on the table. Putting them on their wrists, they noticed that they looked like watch bands. "This good?" Melanie asked.

"Perfect," Xeno replied. "Now, sit down in front of me with the hand you put the bracelet on covering both of your eyes."

Melanie and Emory slowly sat down as they obeyed his commands. "This will only hurt a tiny bit." Xeno said as his deep laugh rang out again.

After he said this, Melanie and Emory felt a shock go into their brain where their hands were. Contrary to what Xeno had said about the pain, it hurt a lot. It felt as if there was lightning being shocked into their brains. Melanie tried to pull her hand away from her face, but couldn't. The two of them grunted in pain, unable to do anything to stop it. About a minute after it started, it had stopped. It felt as if it didn't even happen. Melanie looked over to Emory as she rubbed her other hand over her face. "Now was that so hard?"

Xeno asked them. Something about his voice was different. It didn't have the echo and fade that it normally had. It was coming from someplace different.

Their minds.

Melanie grabbed her chest, unable to believe what had just happened. "What the fuck was that you said it wouldn't hurt!" Emory exclaimed.

"Em, you are focusing on the wrong thing here. We just heard Xeno's voice in our minds."

Emory's eyes widened and fear replaced the pain she was feeling. "That's just step one!" Xeno called out, not in their minds anymore. "But, seeing as you're in a hurry to get out of here, we can finish this tomorrow. Now go before the paramedics arrive at your little bus crash." Xeno smiled.

Melanie and Emory nodded, quickly got up and left the room. While walking through the hallway, Emory said to Melanie "Wait he knows we're not going to be anywhere near here tomorrow right?"

"Well if he's in our minds I'd rather not have him know that." She sounded very defeated and confused as they walked down the hall of the warehouse.

Once out of the warehouse, they started to walk back to the bus, twigs snapping under their feet as they walked quickly. Once they got closer to the bus, they heard the loud sirens of the ambulances, police cars, and fire trucks approaching their location. "Hm, I guess he wasn't lying about calling the paramedics," Melanie whispered.

"Why did we even take that risk?" Emory replied.

"I don't know, we're idiots I guess." Melanie and Emory made their way back to the side of the bus as the ambulances arrived.

Chapter 6

As they started to pull up to the scene of the crash the red and blue flashing lights got bright and the sirens got louder. The tires of the vehicles screeched as they stopped by the crashed bus. Lots of teams of people started quickly going around the bus, its bright yellow exterior now covered in dirt and surrounded by smoke from the engine that had been crushed. "There's two girls over here!" said one of the police officers, running over to Melanie and Emory. "Are you girls alright?" she grabbed onto Melanie and Emory's shoulders as she asked.

"Yeah, we're fine. We're the ones who called you. Everyone else on the bus has passed out I think." Melanie said.

Emory slowly turned to Melanie and started at the side of her face. "We know, we're going to get your classmates to the nearest hospital. They all look mostly fine, the bus driver on the other hand will probably need surgery. I'll take you to my car over there and I'll take you to the hospital so the doctors can do further checks on your girls as they ask you questions, okay?" The woman seemed genuinely concerned for them, but talked to them in a very calm tone.

Melanie and Emory nodded as the woman led them to a police car on the side of the road, not facing the bus. She opened the door and let them in. "I'll be back in a little bit, at least until we know that everyone is out of the crash and being transported to the hospital. You girls are very lucky that you were conscious and able to call for help." The officer then closed the door.

Emory looked at Melanie again "Why did you lie to that officer?" she asked.

"I don't know, I thought it would've been easier than having to say 'Oh yeah some weird demon jackalope-rabbit thing called you guys after we let him into our minds.'" she said mockingly.

Emory sighed and nodded. "Did you have one of those nightmares last night?"

"Yeah, I did," Melanie started, "but this time it was different."

"Different how?"

"I was on the floor, I couldn't move, and I could feel everything that happened." Melanie rested her head on the window of the cop car.

"And what happened?" Emory pushed.

"So, I felt this cold sharp pain at the top of my spine, then it started to go down my spine. Xeno was cutting my back open. Then I felt him open my back and rip my spine out. And then, he grabbed my ribcage and pulled my ribs through my lungs, two at a time. That shit hurt like a fucking bitch." She rolled her eyes.

Emory chuckled a bit. "The hell are you laughing at, I couldn't even scream." Melanie lightly punched Emory in her shoulder.

"Sorry, sorry, it's just," she paused, "you could say he broke your back?" Emory had to try her best to not laugh when she said that.

Melanie's face contorted into one of fear and disgust "You are disgusting." She said annoyed.

"My bad, my bad. But you felt all of it?"

"All of it. And now look where we are." Melanie let out a soft huff of air. "You said you had a nightmare with him in it too?"

"I think it was him, it was just knocking and laughing though. I didn't see anything." Emory spoke calmly.

The car smelled like smoke, in a bad way. There was an air freshener on the rearview mirror, but all it did was add to the bad smell instead of eliminating it. The leather seats were itchy and it wasn't until now that Melanie and Emory had noticed how much they were trembling. The back of the front seats seemed very scratched up, showing the yellow color of the inside of the seat. "Oh my god it smells so bad in here, I can not take it." Emory complained.

"Well, the other option is being passed out in the back of an ambulance." Melanie messed with the phone in her hands, putting one of her headphones back in.

"Are you seriously listening to music right now?" Emory asked.

"what? it calms me down." Melanie said.

"Anyways, If we did pass out we wouldn't have to worry about that Xeno guy."

"Emory, what if Xeno isn't even real."

"He said he was going to make us do stuff? What kind of stuff do you think he means?" Emory continued, not paying any attention to her friend.

Melanie rolled her eyes and didn't even try to repeat herself. "I'm not sure, and I hope that we don't have to find out."

A few minutes later, the cop came back to the car and got into the driver's seat. As the car drove off, Melanie could see the wreckage of the bus through her window. "What are your girl's names?" the officer asked.

"I'm Emory Brooke," She looked over to Melanie and pointed to her, "and that's Melanie Adelia."

"You're in good hands girls, when we get to the hospital I will have to ask you some questions though."

Emory nodded as Melanie continued to stare out the window. The wind blew through the deep green trees, oblivious to what had just happened. It felt like a blink until they were at the hospital, nobody spoke a word, knowing they would be questioned. The officer parked close to the entrance and opened the door to let the girls out. Walking in, they saw all of the ambulances carrying in their unconscious classmates. A tiny bit of Melanie's stomach sank when she saw them, they all looked fine but something about seeing someone she barely knew probably on the verge of death made her heart hurt a little. The officer led Melanie and Emory through the front doors of the hospital and sat them both down in a room. Both of them got their vitals checked and Emory's phone was buzzing like crazy with texts from her mom asking if she was okay. Emory had to quickly respond to all of the messages to not worry her mother more. Melanie's phone, on the other hand, stayed silent. Not even her mom thought to make sure she was okay. It was that she hadn't seen any news on what had happened yet. Once their vitals were checked and everything looked good, the doctors left to call their parents and the officer sat down across from Melanie and Emory. "So girls, I'm going to have to ask you some questions, are you okay with that?" The woman pulled out her clipboard and a pen, ready to write some things down as Melanie and Emory nodded. To Emory, Melanie looked to still be out of it a bit.

The woman looked up at them, "Where were you guys sitting on the bus?"

"We were in the front of it," Emory replied.

"What happened before the bus crashed?"

"The bus was swerving a bit, then it stopped, then we crashed." Emory looked at Melanie as she said this, and Melanie nodded.

"Did the driver seem drunk?" said the officer while writing something down.

"Not really, he looked more tired than drunk."

The officer looked at Emory and then at Melanie, "I believe that is all the questions I have for you girls. Thank you for your honesty." she stood up, "I think your parents are here." She opened the door of the room to the lobby of the hospital where both Melanie and Emory's moms were there, talking with each other, though only Emory's mom looked concerned. Melanie noticed that her mom looked annoyed to be there.

They both went up to their moms "Oh thank god you're okay, what the hell happened?" Emory's mom asked, hugging her daughter.

"The bus crashed into a tree, we were the only ones who didn't pass out." Emory explained what had happened to their moms.

"I'm just so happy you girls are safe, we don't know what we would've done if the call we got was one about you being hurt or worse." Emory's mom put her hand over her chest as she slowed her breathing.

They walked out of the hospital and Melanie went to her mom's car. "So you're not going to say anything?" Melanie asked.

"What's there to ask?" her mom replied coldly.

"I don't know, maybe something like 'Hey Melanie, so happy you're not dead!' would be nice."

Her mom stopped at the light, annoyed with her daughter "I'm happy you're not dead. Happy now?"

"A little," she responded coldly.

"How the hell were you and Emory the only ones who didn't get knocked out? Were you at the very back or something?" her mom asked.

"No, actually we were at the front."

"So other than the driver, you and Emory were the closest to the wheel. Interesting."

"Are you asking if we caused the accident?" Melanie asked, shocked.

"Maybe a little bit. I just find it weird that you girls didn't pass out."

Melanie sat there in shock, not expecting her mom to think that she would have been the one to cause the crash.

Chapter 7

As the car pulled into their driveway and parked, Melanie looked at the time on her phone, 12:36. Melanie got out of the car and slammed the door shut. "Don't slam that door." her mom said.

"Fine!" Melanie said angrily as she went inside the house, her mom following close behind. Melanie quickly walked up the stairs and into her room, sitting down on her bed. She opened up her chat with Emory.

Dude my mom just asked the most stupid question.

What?

Wdym?

She asked me if WE caused the crash.

WHAT?!

IKR!!! I'm so pissed off.

That's so stupid. Like, HOW could we have caused the crash? We were just minding our business and it crashed. Not our fault.

EXACTLY!!!

My mom told me school's canceled tomorrow because of the crash, you wanna come over?

Ofc I do. I don't have anything better to do anyways

Okay cool, see you tomorrow.

Yeah. Omg, I hope that the whole warehouse thing was just a really weird dream.

Omg yeah, that guy was weird af. Why the hell did Bro talk through a TV?

We heard him in our MINDS and both had dreams about him. That's what you're most worried about?

Yeah

Honestly, I'm just praying it was some weird special effects or something

I don't know, it's all too weird

I really wanna try to forget about it lmao

Yeah fr

Anyway, I'll see you tomorrow then.

Bye

Bye bye

Melanie got changed and lay down on her bed, slowly watching the hours pass until the sky started to get dark. It was around 8:08 PM when the sky started to display bright yellows and vibrant oranges. Melanie felt more tired than normal, especially since it was so early. She looked at the bracelet on her arm, making her stomach sink. She had a bad feeling about it but did not want to risk taking it off. This is so fucking stupid. This probably didn't even do anything there. She thought to herself. There was no way that the bracelet was what made them feel the pain they felt in the warehouse, right? Melanie rolled over to her back, opened Google on her phone, and typed: "Can bracelets let people into your mind."

All of the results said "no." which calmed her, just a bit. But everything in her gut was telling her that her situation was different. Around 10 PM, Melanie fell asleep with her phone in her hand, still playing a video. She kept waking up multiple times randomly throughout the night. She could have sworn that she heard inaudible whispers telling her to wake up. Throughout the night, Melanie continued to get annoyed more and more every time she would wake up. After every time she would wake up, it would be exactly an hour from the last.

Chapter 8

In the morning, around 9:00 Am, she woke up for real. She slowly opened her eyes and grabbed her phone, turning it on, she saw a bunch of messages from Emory filling up her screen.

MELANIE!!!

MEL

MEL

MEL

WAKE UP

[attachment: 1 image]

IS THIS THING IN YOUR ROOM TOO?

Huh?

The image that Emory sent was of a weird animal mask. Melanie sat up and looked around her room, confused. When she looked towards her desk with unfinished homework on it, she saw a mask that looked identical to the one Emory sent in the picture. Melanie opened her chat with Emory and sent a picture of it.

[attachment: 1 image]

Wtf...

OH MY GOD

What even is it?

SOME MASK???

No shit Sherlock, what animal is it?

HOW AM I SUPPOSED TO KNOW???

IT HAS LONG EARS AND HORNS WHAT ANIMAL EVEN HAS THAT??

A jackalope...

Wait...

WHAT???

Wasn't Xeno a jackalope or something?

...

Mel... it wasn't a dream, was it...

Realization suddenly set in on what was happening. How the hell could this even be possible? Melanie almost dropped her phone, as her body began to tremble. She walked over to her desk, staring at the mask. "Pick it up." Xeno's voice called, causing Melanie to jump.

She stayed silent, not knowing if she was hallucinating or not. "You heard me, pick it up," he said the last three words slowly.

Melanie reached a hand out to touch the mask, slowly. "I SAID PICK IT UP," he screamed.

Melanie felt her hand quickly gravitate towards the mask, slightly touching it. She didn't move her hand on her own, it felt like something, or, someone moved her hand. "Good, now put it on."

"What..?" she whispered.

"Put. It. On."

Melanie grabbed the mask with her hands and put it on her face. The head strap seemed to grip around her skull. Once it was on, she looked around her room. The world looked different with the mask on. Some parts of the walls, such as doors and windows in her room had indigo-colored mesh covering them. Behind her, she saw a glitchy door in the middle of her room, the frame of which was glowing brightly. "Go through the frame." Melanie felt her body walking towards the door, unable to control herself. Her heart began to beat rapidly.

There was a flash of light when her body went through it. When she opened her eyes, she was back at the warehouse. With the mask on, the warehouse looked so much different. So many more of those doors and rooms that she would have never been able to see. She tumbled over onto the floor, nauseous and unable to keep her balance. She held her hands out in front of her on the floor, keeping her breathing while she tried to not throw up. Then she heard another loud thump on the floor beside her. She looked over to see Emory lying down on her back groaning. "Emory?!" she asked, a mix of shock and surprise.

"Oh shit, you're here too?" Emory asked, wearing the same mask as Melanie and the one she sent in the picture.

"Is this the goddamn warehouse from yesterday?" Melanie asked.

"I mean it looks like it, but with weird purple mesh every-where."

Melanie looked down to the floor and saw wires scattered along the floor, light showing through them as they all connected to the monitor at the back of the room. They looked up at the screen and saw Xeno staring at them. "Now we can talk more about what this means for you two." he smiled.

"How the hell are we even here? This isn't even physically possible!" Melanie yelled.

"It's not. But then again, I'm not really physical am I?" he said, still smiling. "Oh, and you can take the masks off now. I'll tell you more of what they're for in a minute but I'm sure they are hurting your tiny little heads."

Melanie and Emory slowly took off the masks and saw the world go back to its normal, dull state. "I think I'm gonna be sick..." Emory said as she covered her mouth.

Melanie stared at her friend. "If you throw up, do it far away from me."

"I swear to god I'm gonna do it right in your fucking mouth."

"Woah woah Em, we're not freaky like that," Melanie smirked playfully

Emory looked at Melanie with a confused face, "not like that, weirdo. You're disgusting."

Xeno groaned from inside the monitor. "I brought you here for a reason. Now shut up and listen."

"Our bad," Emory said.

"I have been watching you both for a while now. I feel that you would be perfect for what I have planned."

"Planned?" Melanie said

"When we met yesterday, I said that I would be your savior. I also said that that will come with a few tasks from me."

"What kind of tasks?" Melanie asked suspiciously.

"Stuff that my digital self can't do otherwise!"

Melanie raised an eyebrow "Which is?"

"I may or may not have you kill people." Xeno chuckled.

Melanie stood up. "There's no way we're doing that! We'll go to jail."

Xeno closed his eyes and shook his head slightly. "Relax, it's only until I have enough power to free myself from this hell."

"So souls are real," Melanie whispered to herself.

"They're very real, they hold so much power that if you harness enough of it, you can do anything."

"So you want us to get souls for you by killing people? If that's the case then how do you even hold a soul?" Melanie subconsciously took a small step forward.

"If you kill someone with those masks and bracelets on, you would see their soul after they die. It's very simple, my dear."

Emory suddenly spoke up, "And what if we don't? What if we just leave now and never come back? We don't have to do anything you tell us." She smiled.

"I'm afraid I can not allow that." Xeno laughed softly, "If you do, I'll have to make you stay. And trust me, nobody wants that."

"Emory shut up," Melanie grumbled, slowly turning around to face Emory.

"Oh my god, Mel you can't seriously tell me you're thinking about trusting this guy or something, right?"

"Well I have a bad feeling that this is a life or death situation and I don't want to find out by fucking up!"

Xeno smiled, "and you're right about that. This is life or death, as hard as it may be to believe, your life is in my hands."

Melanie turned back around to face Xeno "What do we have to do to not die then?" Melanie sounded aggravated and angry.

"Like I said, kill people that I tell you to. Those people would probably be people who get close to finding out about our existence and what I am making you do, and people who are distracting you from our ultimate goal of freeing me."

"Oh my god, I need a minute," Emory said with a lot of air in her lungs.

Melanie watched her friend stand up and pace around the room, trying to breathe.

"You do know that we are two fifteen-year-old girls who have never even touched a sharp object before in their lives and you expect us to murder people?" Melanie put a lot of volume on the last part of her sentence.

"I'll guide you through your first few, just until you get the hang of it."

Emory stopped pacing around and looked at Xeno. "How do you know what you're doing? You're just some stupid computer program."

"Funny thing is, I was human once, like you. But I had gained enough power through my killings that I was able to come back as this creature. You can free me and let me roam this earth. And in return, you will gain my help and knowledge of anything. I'm basically a half-dead supercomputer."

Melanie and Emory stayed silent, not knowing what to say. How could this projection on a screen ever have been human, or even get into their minds?

"May I also mention that there will be rules that you must follow to ensure both of you make it out of this unharmed?"

"What kind of rules?" Melanie asked.

"Let me list them for you." Xeno smiled once again, his smile seemed as if it could pierce through a thick block of ice. Xeno's screen flashed to a screen that had a list of rules on it, reading them off as the list went down. "Number one, you must do as I say without any questions. Number two, failure to complete a task within the time frame given will result in punishment. Number three, if a bond with another human gets in the way of your work for me, you will have to kill them without them knowing. Number four, whatever happens, I will always be here to guide you. Do you understand?"

Melanie stepped back to stand next to Emory, "Too late to back out now." Melanie whispered.

Emory sighed then turned back to Xeno, "We understand."

"I'm very happy that you agree. We will talk more later, you are free to leave."

"Uhm, about that, how do we leave?" Emory asked.

"Same way you came, put on the mask, think about where you want to go, and the door will take you there. I will inform you when to come back next."

Melanie and Emory put on the masks again, the world shifting to the weird glitchy purple world. They looked behind them and found a door, both going through it and finding themselves back in their rooms after the flash of light faded away. A few seconds later Melanie received a text from Emory.

Come over to my house as soon as you can. We need to talk about whatever the fuck just happened

Okay but promise me we're not going to try and anger the bitchy jackalope demon?

Oh my god

Why would we? he's scary

You acted like a pussy back there btw

what? Did not!

Uh-huh

you totally did.

I just had a normal human reaction, that's all.

I mean he seems nice if you ignore the whole killing thing

Oh my god, are you serious, psycho? Just get over here.

Maybe if we don't piss him off and just do what he says then he'll help us with our homework.

You're so fucking sick. And I thought you were against murder in general/

Yeah, I am, but Xeno said it was life or death, and I want to at least try to live until my 30's

Just get over here!

Okay, okay, I'll be there in like ten minutes.

As Melanie got changed, she heard her phone buzz again, this time when she looked, it was an alert message that said "always watching :)" She stared at it for a minute before deciding to swipe it away.

She ran down the stairs "Bye Mom, I'm going over to Emory's house, I'll be home soon."

"Okay, stay safe." her mom responded.

Melanie grabbed her bike and rode over to Emory's house. When she got there, she rang the doorbell and waited for someone to answer. A few seconds after she rang it, the front door opened and Emory stood there. "Let's go to my room, my older brother's still asleep I think."

Emory used to have a younger brother too, that was until he got killed a little over two years ago in a shooting. He was out with his friend and that friend's mom to see a movie. Some psycho, Emory's words, not hers, came into the theater, pulled out a gun, and just started shooting. Melanie didn't know any of the major details. All she remembered was how much Emory cried through the days and weeks after it happened. Emory still cried about it sometimes, not just because he was her brother, but because of how young he was. He had his whole future ahead of him, and so did his friend. Melanie swore she heard Emory sniffle as they passed the deceased boy's room. She went into Emory's room with her and sat down on her bed. Her yellow walls were decorated with pictures of her and her family. The room itself brought a very warm vibe to anybody who walked in it, it was almost calming. Melanie sat across from Emory on her bed. "Jesus Christ, what did we get ourselves into?" Emory asked.

"Something bad, that's for sure." Melanie replied.

"You do realize that I can hear what you are saying whenever I please, correct?" Xeno asked, in their minds.

"Shit he can do what now?" Melanie whispered to Emory. Xeno didn't respond.

"Well, now we have to be careful with what we say too?" Emory asked, annoyed.

"I guess, but hey, it's all going to be fine, right? We have each other. Remember when we were in seventh grade and Megan left us for stupid Brittany? You were so upset and all I said to cheer you up was that we still had each other."

"Mel, that's not the same."

"I know it's not the same but it's still true."

Emory stayed silent for a second "I'm confused about why you started having nightmares about Xeno two months and I only had one the night before the crash." she said.

"I'm confused about that as well." Melanie said, trying to think.

"Do you think this is going to be the rest of our lives?" Emory asked

"No, no it won't be. It can't take too long for him to get the power he needs, right? We'll just have to wait it out. We will get through this, okay?" Melanie swung her legs off of Emory's bed and walked around.

"What are you doing?" Emory asked her.

"Where did you put that mask?" Melanie asked back.

"Just on the dresser over there, why?"

Melanie went over to Emory's dresser and grabbed the mask "Because we need to hide these."

"Why though," Emory started, "why do we need to hide them?"

"If you had a kid and just found a weird mask in their room after a bus crash, you'd start asking questions, too, right?" Melanie said as she grabbed the mask and put it in Emory's closet.

"Right..." Emory said as she watched Melanie.

Melanie closed Emory's closet and sat back down on the bed. "Maybe it won't be that bad. Hell, maybe we'll even like it."

Emory kept her eyes on Melanie "You're joking."

"What does it look like?" Melanie said as she pinched the bridge of her nose

"Mel, there's no way we can do this."

"How are we supposed to stop it then? It's not like we can do anything about it." Melanie put her hand on her leg.

Emory started to fidget with the purple bracelet "I know that we can't do anything about it but-"

Melanie cut her off, "Em, we fucking teleported from our houses to that damn warehouse. If you say one thing about how this could still just be a 'bad dream' we are far past that point."

Emory sighed softly, "I know that, but it's just all too hard to believe. It happened so fast."

"For you maybe, but I've had those nightmares for two months before the crash yesterday."

Emory stayed quiet, unable to say anything. She then slowly nodded, looking around her room. "You wanna do something? It's a day off for us so we might as well use it."

"Imagine being in the hospital instead of having the day off." Melanie looked over to a wall.

"Is that a yes?" she raised an eyebrow

"Of course it is," Melanie said, looking back at Emory.

They spent the rest of the day laughing, playing games, and watching TV together. The hours passed quickly, they didn't even notice that the sun had gone down. Melanie left

Emory's house just before the sun had fully gone down. While riding back home, she had her headphones on, casually listening to music. She didn't ride while listening to music often, but she felt calmer with it.

Chapter 9

The weekend ended almost faster than it had started. It felt like when she fell asleep on Friday, she woke up inside the school. Sitting down at the desk next to Emory, she looked around the classroom and noticed that every single one of their classmates were back from the hospital and looked like it had never happened. One or two students that were behind the two of them had a few scratches on their upper arms, but that was pretty much it. "Did you hear that Mr. David is in jail?" One of their classmates whispered to another.

"No, really?" another student replied.

Melanie looked around the room and whispered to Emory, "Who the hell is Mr. David?"

"The bus driver that crashed the bus. I think he's in there for a year." Emory said as if she was talking to a five-year-old. Melanie's jaw dropped to the floor upon hearing this. "What did you think was going to happen? He crashed a bus full of school kids."

"I don't know what I thought would happen. I just didn't think that he could go to jail at all since nobody got hurt." Melanie shrugged.

"He got charged with child endangerment. When he gets out, I doubt he's ever going to have a license again."

Later that day in physics class, Melanie watched as the red-haired girl walked into the classroom, looked at Ms. Lodge, and yelled "I told you so!"

Ms. Lodge just sighed and told the girl to take a seat. "I think since all of you just got out of the hospital, I'm just going to keep this class easy today."

"Are there gonna be any paper worksheets? Because my arm still kinda hurts." one boy asked.

"No no, I'm just going to tell you a story that may or may not be fictional."

The class looked at Ms. Lodge with confusion-stricken faces. "Have any of you heard about the curse of the jacka-lope?" she asked, a small smile across her face.

"No? What even is a jackalope?" one student asked.

Damn, we really need better education here. Melanie thought.

"Oh my god Kyle, there's no way you're serious." Ms. Lodge said as she rubbed her forehead. "Anyway, a jackalope is a cross between an extinct pygmy-deer and a rabbit. The curse however is said to have been started in the eighties, almost forty years ago. People say that the curse starts with recur-ring nightmares that sometimes last for months on end."

"That just sounds like trauma instead of a curse." one girl said as she rolled her eyes.

"What was that thing your math teacher always tells you to say? 'But wait, there's more?'" she laughed.

"No, there's nothing other than PTSD there." the girl continued to argue.

"Oh my god Sally, just let Ms. Lodge tell the story." multiple people said.

"Okay okay fine." the girl rolled her eyes.

Ms. Lodge coughed to get everyone's attention again. "As I was saying, the nightmares would last for months on end to whom the jackalope sees as 'worthy'. One night the nightmare will change into something that hurts more than anything that the victim had felt before. Whatever it is, it's supposed to resemble the blood eagle torture method from medieval times."

"Isn't that where someone pulls your ribs out of your back to look like wings?" the redhead asked.

Ms. Lodge nodded. "That's exactly what it is and from what I've heard it can vary in different ways, sometimes the jackalope will pull their ribs out through their lungs."

Most of the class looked disgusted as Ms. Lodge spoke. Melanie looked over to Emory and mouthed what the fuck. "The next thing that happens is actually what made me want to tell you guys this story."

"What, was there a bus crash or something?" Kyle asked as he laughed.

"Actually, yes. The next thing that supposedly happens is that the victim, or in some cases victims get involved in some way with a bus crash. Then, the jackalope will take over its victim's mind and make whoever it is do whatever he says, without question. But, thankfully, it's just a story of fiction."

"Doesn't sound like fiction," Emory whispered to Melanie.

"Sounds like reality," Melanie whispered back.

"It's a miracle that you're all alive with barely getting hurt." Ms. Lodge said as she looked over to Melanie and Emory as they whispered to each other in the back of the classroom.

"Oh my god Melanie we're cursed." Emory panicked.

"Calm down, it's not a curse- " Melanie got cut off.

"Then what would you call it?"

"Something that you'd like to share with the class?" Ms. Lodge asked them.

Melanie and Emory's heads shot up to look at Ms. Lodge. "Uhm, no ma'am." Melanie trailed off.

"That's what I thought," she said and turned back to sit down.

"She doesn't have to be such a bitch." Melanie whispered.

"This is boring. Is this really what you do all day?" Xeno's deep voice rang.

Melanie and Emory let out a small scream in unison. Quickly covering their mouths after. They felt everyone's eyes locking on them. "Our bad.." Emory said, everyone's heads turned back around, away from them.

"What the fuck?" Melanie muttered angrily, raising her tone with the last word, her voice cracking slightly.

"Answer me," Xeno said.

"I don't know?!" she felt her heart beating fast, slightly shaking and breathing heavily.

No response.

"Did you see them in physics today? Oh my god, it was super weird, they both looked like lunatics I swear."

Melanie looked to the right of her to see a group of girls talking about her and Emory. "Just ignore them, Mel." Emory said.

"I can't, though. I'm sorry we had a normal human reaction to something." Melanie poked at the chicken on her lunch tray. "Do you think this is poison?"

Emory looked down to the chicken on both of their trays "It tastes like some sort of ant killer, but I don't think it can kill a human."

"And you know what ant killer tastes like?" Melanie raised an eyebrow.

"No, ugh, you know what I mean." Emory put her hand up to her forehead.

"No, no, they practically fell out of their seats oh my god I would jump out of a window if I was them." one of the girls said, causing everyone else in their group to laugh.

Melanie took a sip of her water, "God, I can't wait to graduate."

Emory finished chewing "We still have over two years of this."

She groaned, "Why did we go here anyway? What were we thinking?"

"To get away from Megan, but that didn't go as well as we hoped. Plus, our parents thought that it would be good for us to get some 'God in us'. Some stupid shit like that." Emory coughed, "I'm gonna throw up if I eat any more of this."

"Then stop eating it." Melanie put her head in her hand. "I wish that crash killed Megan, maybe Brittany too but it's whatever."

"Didn't you say your mom blamed you for the crash? If someone died, especially someone that we kind of hate, wouldn't that just raise more suspicion that you did it?"

"Maybe, but it's not like she would do anything if I did do it."

"She could send you away."

Melanie rolled her eyes "Yeah right, if she sent me away who would she yell at for no reason?"

"That's a fair point." Emory pushed her tray to the side of the table with one of her hands.

The laughing from the other table got louder and more obnoxious. "I swear, I'm going to shove that fork down their fucking throat-" Melanie got cut off by an immense pain coming from her left arm. "Fuck, what is that?" she groaned in pain as she grabbed onto it.

"What are you talking about?" Emory asked, she then suddenly grabbed onto her arm too.

The pain almost felt worse than anything either of them had ever experienced in their entire life. Melanie lifted her sleeve to see brightly colored lines slowly crawling up her arm. The lines seemed to almost resemble cracks and glowed in a bright indigo color. She also noticed the purple bracelet that she and Emory got from the warehouse. "Em, I think it's coming from those bracelets." Melanie quickly put her sleeve down to not have anybody notice the brightly colored cracks.

"Wait what?" Emory said, lifting her sleeve to see the same cracks that Melanie saw. Her eyes widened as she slowly put down her sleeve. "But these hurt, like really bad." Emory winced. "Are you sure?"

"It's happening to both of us at the same time, it's never happened before, and it's only on the arm that that stupid bracelet thing is on." Melanie's tone shifted into one of panic and concern, something she didn't do often.

Emory noticed Melanie's frantic state, "Stop panicking, If you panic, then I'm going to start panicking too!"

"Stop panicking," Xeno spoke, sounding almost annoyed.

Melanie and Emory both jumped slightly, just like they had earlier. They let out a small scream again, "Stop." Emory said through her hands which were covering her mouth, dragging out the end of the word.

"It's not like it's going to kill you or anything, just cause a bit of pain, that's all." He lightly chuckled at the end of his sentence.

"Oh my god look, they did it again." a girl from the other table said, clearly trying not to be heard but failing.

Emory groaned, "Well, can you make it stop? Melanie isn't handling the pain well and I'm not either!"

Xeno moved on to a completely different thought, "Wow those girls over there are assholes."

"Tell me about it." Melanie said through gritted teeth as she gripped her arm.

Emory let out a fake dramatic cough.

"Oh right, I will, just meet me later today when you can." After Xeno said this, the pain in their arms slowly stopped as the cracks retreated down. Melanie slowly let go of her arm, lifting her sleeve as the cracks inched further down her arm until they were gone completely. "I'll speak with you two later."

Suddenly, one of the girls at the other table began choking, her face turning slightly purple. Xeno laughed, but it stopped abruptly as he left.

"Oh my god, Kimmy!" one of the girls shouted.

"Kimmy's choking! Oh my gosh Tiffany, what do we do?" another one of them said frantically.

"Uhm, I don't know! Help! Someone help! Kimmy's Choking!" the Tiffany girl yelled. Melanie couldn't help but giggle slightly.

The rest of their classmates started to worry, standing up from their seats to get a better look at what was going on. There weren't too many people having lunch at that time, it was maybe about fifty people in total. They were all muttering to each other, not sure what was going on. Some spoke in a worried tone, others not so much.

One of the cafeteria staff members quickly came over and gave Kimmy the Heimlich maneuver. She quickly stopped choking, but nothing came up from her throat other than a tiny amount of a black, tar-like substance that had hints of purple in the light. "Gosh, ew Kimmy, you fattie! You scared us half to death!" Kimmy just looked at her friends with a confused look. The staff member who helped Kimmy out just walked away.

"Hey," the girl who first spoke when Kimmy began to choke began, "Was Melanie laughing when she saw Kimmy choking? Did she have something to do with it?" she asked.

Tiffany turned to Melanie and then back to her friend, "how would she have something to do with it? She's all the way over there, dummy."

Melanie turned her head to Kimmy, then to Emory. "You don't think that,"

"What? That it was this nasty school food? Yeah, you're probably right." Emory shrugged.

"Oh my god, no. Xeno said that they were assholes and laughed right after 'Kimmy' started choking." Melanie said. 'Kimmy''s real name was Kimberly, but people just called her Kimmy for short because they couldn't be bothered. Nobody even asked if she liked the nickname, they just started to call her that randomly one day and it just kept growing and growing until people started to think that Kimmy was her actual name.

"You're not saying he did that right? I mean he couldn't possibly," Emory paused to think for a moment, "Okay, maybe he did."

A little while after school ended, Melanie found herself in the same warehouse from the other day, staring at Emory who was already sitting down on the ground. It looked like she had been waiting there for a little while. The monitor at the back of the room turned on, "Finally, watching you go through those hellish school lessons was boring me out." Xeno said, annoyed.

"Yeah well they bore us out too, and what the fuck were those weird lines about earlier? And why did they hurt so much?" Melanie asked.

Emory turned around, "Oh hey, when did you get here?" she asked.

"Just now," Melanie said bluntly as she sat down next to Emory. She placed her mask down on the floor next to her, she noticed that Emory had done the same thing.

"They were just to get your attention, but I forgot that I had not told you that yet. They're nothing to be afraid of, not unless you're in trouble." Xeno stated.

"Trouble?" Melanie asked, confused.

"Yeah, when you disobey, fail my tasks, or dare defy me. That's the only time that those little cracks will get much more painful than they were today." he smiled menacingly.

"They can get more painful?" Melanie asked.

"Of course they can!" Xeno uttered. "Earlier today I was going to have you two do something, but I then remembered that I hadn't taught you girls anything yet. Matter of fact, that's what I plan to do today."

"Great, more learning." Emory groaned slightly.

Xeno ignored Emory, "The only way you can teleport is with those masks on, having those masks on is also what lets you create portals to other places. I realized that you both do not keep your masks near you at all times, but you won't need to. There's a very simple way to summon them. You see, hand movements are sort of the 'key to the universe', or at least one of them. I made it that way so when I finally found people like you two it would be much easier."

"Wait, wait, wait, back up, what do you mean by you made it that way?" Melanie asked.

"I made the universe that way, it's very simple."

"So what are you? Are you like," Melanie paused for a second, "a god?"

"You're smart and correct."

"Oh shit we're working for god, we are so fucked" Emory said, nervously laughing, unable to believe what she had heard.

"Wait, you're joking, right? You have to be joking." Melanie said, her voice slightly breathy."

"I thought I told you this already, did I not?" Xeno asked.

"No?!" Melanie and Emory said in unison.

"Hm, I could've sworn that I did. Anyways, apologies for sort of dropping that on you two." Xeno took a brief pause before he continued stating what he was talking about before. "As I was saying, I made hand movements one of the keys to the universe. It allows you to do basically anything you want, well at least some cool things."

"Okay hold on, we need you to pause. So, you're saying you are god. Does that mean all of the other religions aren't true?" Melanie asked.

"Religion was made through evolution, I could have had control over it if I wanted to, but I simply did not and instead let everything take its course. I like to think everything happens for a reason." Xeno answered.

"Oh my god Mrs. J's gonna be so pissed when she finds that out," Emory smirked.

Melanie laughed slightly. "Wait, so why do you need us?"

His eyes darkened, "Because, I want control over it again. And I am too weak to do it by myself. I simply do not have the strength. But while you help me get the strength and power back that I need, nobody is allowed to know what we are doing. Not your family, not your friends, nobody. Especially not the cops or government. Do I make myself clear?" Xeno raised his voice near the end of his sentence, it was almost like a warning.

Melanie and Emory nodded.

"But you're God, Xeno. don't you want people to know about your existence?" Emory asked.

"Oh, believe me, I would love it. But all of you humans think that there's something greater out there after death, but there isn't. And last time someone found out about me, it caused a whole religious war on who's right and who's wrong, if I'm real or not, and I do not want to fix that again." he spoke in an annoyed tone.

"This isn't making any sense," Melanie said.

"It will begin to make sense very soon, my dear. Let's just get back to what I was going to show you." Xeno's screen suddenly flashed with glitchy hands on the screen. The hands had very large claws, something about the overall look of them gave Melanie a bad feeling in her stomach. There was no way that these hands were computer generated, they were too fluid, too much like a human. They had to be the hands of Xeno. Melanie noticed that they seemed to have lines of binary code that were not opaque at all but still able to be barely seen. As Melanie studied them, she felt like she had seen them somewhere before. Her mind flashed to the night that she had seen a figure behind her in her mirror, forcefully holding her down by the shoulder, almost digging into her skin. The hands began to make motions that looked like they could have been gang signs. "This 'hand-code' as I call it, will let you summon your masks whenever you need."

The hands went slowly, making sure to clearly show each part of the hand code. The hand movements on the screen stopped, "do you think you got that?" Xeno asked.

"Uhm, maybe?" Melanie said.

"Try it, Melanie. Go to the other side of the room and try it." Xeno said sternly.

Melanie stood up, leaving her mask next to Emory as she walked to the other side of the room. As she stood, she slowly began to do the hand code, very slowly at first, trying to remember all of it. After she finished the last part of it, her mask fell at her feet. "Holy shit."

"Very good, very good." Xeno sounded pleased. "Now you try it, Emory."

Emory stood up and walked over to where Melanie was standing, she took notice of how shocked Melanie looked. "Mel, are you good? You look like you just saw a ghost." Emory asked.

"No, no I'm fan-fucking-tastic. I'm just in shock, how the hell did I do that?"

Emory laughed a bit as she began to do the hand code, just as slowly as Melanie. After she finished, the same thing happened. "Oh my God, that's cool as fuck!" Emory exclaimed.

"You girls both have potential in you, it's exciting to see." Xeno continued to sound very pleased. "There's one last thing I have to teach you today, and that's how to make portals. It's quite easy, all you have to do is think about where you want the portal to lead to, and then with two fingers, you draw a door frame. Then It just appears, only being able to be closed by me or one of you two. Hell, it's so easy that you're free to go home, I trust you'll remember how to do it when the time comes, correct?"

Melanie finally picked up her mask from the floor, "Uhm, yeah, I guess."

"Good, you're free to leave. And if you need me, just say my name, I'll be watching," he said as the monitor turned off.

Emory put on her mask, "Shit do you know if we have any tests tomorrow?"

"Don't you keep track of all of our tests and stuff?"

"Yeah, but I'm just double-checking in case I missed something."

Melanie put on her mask as well, "well you're asking the wrong person."

"You're right, well, I'll see you tomorrow," Emory said as she stepped through one of the portals. Melanie did the same thing and she was back in her room. She took off the mask and put it back in her closet.

Chapter 10

As the hours passed, Melanie couldn't stop thinking about the slightly opaque lines of code on Xeno's hands, something about them worried her. "Xeno?" she asked quietly.

"What is it, Melanie?" Xeno asked from inside of Melanie's head.

"Earlier, were those hands you showed us yours?"

"Yes, they were. Why?"

"I noticed that there were lines of code on them. It was very faded but it was there, does it mean anything?"

"You were always so observant, I've noticed that for a while."

"A while?"

"I told you that I've been watching you for a long time, years now. I know how you work, what makes you angry, and happy, everything about you. You always were observant in everything. That code you noticed is what I am made of, it's what everything is made of. Everything is made of code, from each blade of grass to every single mountain."

"But, the only things that have everything made of code are simulations," Melanie replied confused.

"That's what all of this is. Everything works just like a computer that only some can access."

"So, does that mean there's nothing after we die?"

"Think of it like the trash file on a computer, the files are just there to waste away. You become nothing, just a small file of human waste."

"Is that it? It's just nothing?" Melanie asked. "there's seven minutes of brain activity after death, though. Something has to happen in that time."

"That brain activity is what allows you to pass on, to become nothing." Melanie stayed quiet after hearing this. "Is that all?" Xeno asked.

"Yes, it is. Thank you."

Once Xeno's voice left, Melanie looked around her room, trying to take in everything he had said. Her eyes landed on a picture of her uncle, who had passed away in a motorcycle accident a few years back. The words "You become nothing" echoed in her head. She was never close to her uncle, nor did she ever really know him, but he was still family. Melanie put her headphones on and listened to music, eventually falling asleep without even realizing it.

Melanie woke up in the morning to see a glass cup, broken on her floor. She groaned as she slid out of bed, not knowing how it got there. As she kneeled down to pick up the broken shards of glass, she rotated her hand in a circle, something that she always did before beginning to pick up things. She then paused as she looked down. The glass shards floated slightly off the ground. "What the hell?" Melanie screamed as she jumped back on the group. The glass then fell back down to the floor and Melanie looked at her hand. "Did I do that?" She asked herself. She then slowly stood up, staring at the pile of glass, "No, no there's no way." Melanie walked closer to it, rotating her hand over it like she did before. The glass began levitating above the ground again, it followed her hand as Melanie moved her arm around.

At school, she saw Emory with a cut on her right cheek, it somehow looked good next to her medium-brown hair. Melanie sat down in her seat across from Emory. "Oh my god, what happened?" Melanie asked.

Emory looked up from her laptop, "Never rotate your hand in a circle in front of a mirror. I did it this morning, the mirror shattered, and one of the glass shards cut my face."

Melanie's eyes widened, "The same thing happened to me! Well, not quite but there was a broken glass cup on the floor of my room and you know how I rotate my hand before picking up anything? Yeah, well I did that and the glass just started levitating under my hand."

Emory groaned, "What the hell have we gotten ourselves into?" she put her hands over her face. "Why Glass, though? I tried it over a pencil in my room and nothing happened."

"I might know, a few days before the crash, I looked at my reflection and something was holding me down. Yesterday when Xeno was showing us that hand code thing, I recognized his hands."

"Your point?" Emory asked, slightly confused.

"Mirrors are made out of glass, and if he can show himself in mirrors, it makes sense that we can manipulate glass." Melanie watched as it finally clicked in Emory's head.

"Oh, that makes a lot more sense than I initially thought it would." Emory said as she looked back down to her laptop.

Later that day, Melanie was sitting in the school's religion class, across from Emory. "Remember guys, we have a quiz tomorrow, so don't forget to study the notes we've been going over." Mrs. J said.

Melanie tapped her pencil on the desk, resting her head on her other hand, not paying much attention. Why is all of this happening? What did Em and I do to have this happen? She thought to herself. She heard Emory cough and looked up. Emory pointed to the board with her finger. Melanie sighed as she looked over to the board, she didn't have a good grade in this class and any quiz or test that she would take would just make her grade drop even more. She was holding on to passing by a very low C. "Are you actually gonna study this time?" Emory asked her.

"Yeah, maybe. But I'll probably still fail anyway." Melanie rolled her eyes.

"Don't be too hard on yourself, I'm sure it won't be too bad. Just go over the notes from class."

Melanie continued to tap her pencil on her desk, trying to pay a bit more attention to the class. After Mrs. J had finished speaking, she allowed the class free time to study for the quiz tomorrow, something she always did.

At home, Melanie sat on her bed, thinking about whether she should study or not. She knew that it would have probably been a good idea too, but she didn't feel like getting up and trying to remember a bunch of random things. "Melanie!" she heard her mom yell from downstairs.

"Yeah?" she yelled back

"Get down here!"

Shit, shit, shit, shit, shit, what could she have possibly done? Was it the cup from that morning? The Xeno thing? Her mind raced as she slowly stepped down the stairs, preparing herself. When she got downstairs, she saw her mom sitting down on the couch with an angry expression. "Yeah, mom? What is it?"

"You're practically failing that damn religion class!" she exclaimed.

"It's a C, though! And it's not like it's going to help me out in the real world anyway!" Melanie replied.

"Yes, but it's an easy class! There's no reason for you not to have an A! Is there any way that you can get credit fast? The school year is almost over."

"I have a quiz tomorrow-" Melanie tried to explain but got cut off.

"I swear to god Melanie, you better ace that shit."

"I can try, but it's hard material! Especially because Mrs. J. doesn't know how to teach."

"It shouldn't be! Now go to your room and study!"

"But mom!"

"I don't want to fucking hear it! Now go!"

Melanie turned around and walked up to her room, grumbling to herself. She went into her room and sat down at her desk, pulling out her notes. She stared at the questions before pulling out her phone.

Em, help me

Why? U good?

No, Mom's making me study because I'm almost failing

And?

I don't know how to study!

The fuck do you mean you don't know how to study???

Just help me :(

Repeat the questions and answers in your head until you know them.

:(

Melanie set her phone down next to her, looking at her notes again. "I am so fucked." she whispered to herself.

"They're teaching you lies." Xeno suddenly spoke.

"What?" Melanie asked. She noticed that she didn't jump when she suddenly heard his voice as if she was getting used to it happening.

"About death. There's no heaven, no hell, just nothing, remember?"

Melanie didn't want to remember. "Oh, right."

"Why do humans teach this anyway? Just filling their heads with lies."

"If I don't learn this, I'm gonna fail, and if I fail I get yelled at."

Xeno just laughed at this, "I promise you it won't be bad if you," He paused, "fail."

"How would you know?" Melanie asked, her eyes scanning over her notes frantically.

"That is for me to know."

Melanie grunted in annoyance and banged her head on her table. "Fuck it, I think I studied enough, I'll just cheat off

Emory if I have to." Melanie said as she stood up, cleaned up her desk, and went to lie down in her bed.

As the hours passed, the sky darkened and Melanie began to get a bit hungry. She went downstairs and noticed that her mom had fallen asleep on the couch, again. She looked in the pantry only to find microwavable rice bowls. She heated one up and went back to her room. Eventually, Melanie felt her eyes begin to get heavy. With each blink that she took, it felt like it was getting harder and harder to open them back up. Against her attempts to try and stay awake, she fell asleep.

"You studied, right?" Emory asked as they walked into the religion classroom.

"Well, not really. I tried though, so I should be fine."

"Yesterday you were freaking out."

"I'm just a girl. Can't I have a change of heart?" Melanie whipped her head slightly to get the hair out of her face.

Emory rolled her eyes "Sure..."

The two of them sat down in their seats, putting all of their things under their chairs, standard test and quiz procedure. As Melanie sat down, she got a sinking feeling in her stomach. She had been nervous many times before, but nothing like this. "If you studied at all, this quiz will be easy." Mrs. J said as she passed out the quiz papers. "You can begin when you get your paper."

Melanie wrote her name down at the top of her paper before looking down at the questions. She swore quietly under her breath, tapping her pencil on her desk. She could feel her pencil beginning to slip out of her palms which were becoming sweaty.

Emory tried to put her hand on Melanie's shoulder but got shocked in the process. "What the fuck is happening?" Emory whispered to Melanie.

"How should I know?!" Melanie whispered back.

"Girls!" Mrs. J. yelled angrily, "No talking during a test!" some of the class laughed at her outburst.

"Uhm, Mrs. J, I don't think Melanie is feeling too well, can I take her to the office?"

Mrs. J. didn't even look up, she just merely nodded. Emory quickly motioned for Melanie to follow her, which she did. Emory tried to grab her hand to pull her faster, but instead got shocked. "What the fuck is going on with you?" she asked, looking back at her while still quickly walking.

Melanie looked at Emory "I don't know! It just started happening." she said in a panic, looking around her.

Emory pulled her into the bathroom, not many people went in there during class time. "Why is this happening? What is that shit?""It feels like static electricity or something. Like when you rub a balloon on your hair and it stands up." Melanie tapped the top of her hands on the palm of the other rapidly. "It honestly kind of hurts."

"Well, how do you stop it? Whatever it is." Emory asked, "Because I think if someone saw you like that you would be locked up in a lab so fast."

"Get her to calm down, she's stressed. That is what is causing it."

"Holy fuck stop randomly talking out of nowhere!" Emory yelled with a mix of annoyance and anger.

"If you get her to calm down though, the sparks will stop."

Melanie tried to breathe, slow and deep. Calming herself. She felt what was happening to her begin to stop. "What the hell was that?" she asked.

"You tell me, it happened to you," Emory said, still confused. "Are you okay though?"

"Oh, yeah, I'm fine. It's not like it hurt or anything, it just felt kind of weird." Melanie said as she leaned her body against one of the walls.

"It is caused by emotions," Xeno began, "emotions hold more power than humans think. Any strong emotions, negative or positive, cause the body to create electrical currents."

"Everybody has strong emotions at times, so why did that 'electrical current' show up around Melanie?" Emory asked, gesturing towards her friend.

"Because you both work for me now, you're on a higher level of sight than normal people. You can see when it happens to others, but they can't see it when it happens at all."

"I'm sorry, work for you?" Emory asked with a hint of confusion in her voice.

"You work for me until you prove that you can work with me. Working with me is something that you will earn."

Melanie continued to breathe deeply, her hand over her chest to check her heart rate. "You never thought to tell us any of this?"

"The point is for you to find out on your own. Plus, I find that it is more," he paused," entertaining that way." he let out a low chuckle.

Melanie knew that that was not why "Fuck it, let's go back to class, Mel." Emory said as she walked out of the bathroom,

Melanie followed close behind her. "Why did you freak out that much over one of Mrs. J's quizzes?" Emory asked as they walked down the hallway.

"My mom got super pissed at me last night because I'm close to failing the class." Melanie rolled her eyes.

"So is that why you panicked? You studied though, right?"

"Well, a little, but I got distracted." Melanie shrugged. "And the quiz was about death so that might be why."

"I will just come up with answers I think she would like. Pull it out of my ass, y'know?"

Emory knocked on the door to the classroom with Melanie behind her, soon getting let in by one of their classmates.

After school, Melanie sat in the car waiting for her mom to drive off. "Did you do well on that quiz?" her mom asked, not even bothering to look at Melanie.

"Yeah, I think so." Melanie replied quietly.

"Do you know how you did?"

Melanie felt annoyed pulling at her brain "No, Mom, I don't know my grade for two weeks, maybe more. Mrs. J. takes forever to grade our stuff."

"Sorry, how would I know?" her mom said as she drove off. While driving home, her mom spoke up again. "People could have died in that crash."

Melanie turned her head to face her "Excuse me?"

"You heard me."

"Jeez Mom, do you think I could have done anything about it?" she asked, slightly aggravated.

"I'm just saying..." her mom continued to drive.

Melanie turned her head again to look out the window, staring out of it. The houses seemed to blur as they continued driving. Tiny water droplets began to fall from the sky when the car pulled into the driveway. Rain fell on Melanie as she walked into the house. She changed out of her uniform and lay down, sighing as she did. She stared at her ceiling, the only movement she made was the rise and fall of her chest with every breath she took. Her mind took over her body, allowing her to just lay there, feeling numb. Hours seemed to pass like minutes without her even noticing. Suddenly her phone began to ring, she sat up and noticed that the sun had already started to go down. Grabbing her phone, she saw the name Emory at the top of the screen. She quickly pressed the answer button.

"Hello?"

"Hey, yeah, where the fuck are you?" Emory asked with a bit of urgency in her voice.

"What do you mean? Was there some stupid school thing we had to go to?"

"No, dumbass, the warehouse. I've been trying to reach you for the past 30 minutes! Xeno's getting kind of pissed." Emory trailed off.

"Shit, my bad. I didn't know." Melanie slowly got up from her bed.

"How did you not hear or feel anything? How deep asleep were you?"

"I don't even know what I was doing," she said in a breathy voice.

"Okay just please get here, like right now."

Emory hung up the phone and Melanie walked over to her closet where she had put the mask, grabbed it, and put it on.

She noticed that she was getting more used to walking through the portals, barely wobbling now as she stepped through.

"Finally," Xeno grumbled as he saw Melanie come in.

"Sorry, sorry. I didn't know you needed us." Melanie apologized.

"Do not let it happen again," Xeno said sternly. Melanie nodded in response. There was a small pause of awkward silence.

"Are you going to explain why you needed us now?" Emory finally spoke up.

"Ah, yes, thank you for reminding me." Melanie noticed that Xeno sounded... sort of excited? It didn't make any sense to her. "Your first task from me is to kill someone, anyone. It can be some homeless person on the street or a famous rich person, though that may be a little harder. I need you to bring me back their souls."

"I'm sorry, their soul?" Emory asked, confused.

"Yes, soul collection. You will kill someone and collect their soul. It will make all of us more powerful."

Melanie felt her heart drop from fear. There was no way a god was telling them to kill someone right? "How do we even collect their souls? It's physically impossible." Emory crossed her arms.

"I will guide you two through it. I assure you that it will not be hard at all when you get used to it." Xeno seemed to smile. Melanie knew that something about this wasn't right. "I can see that from your memories you two used to run, terribly it seems, but it is something that we can work off of."

Melanie began laughing slightly. "No, there's no way that you will get me running again. That was hell and it hurt like a bitch."

"Silly girl, you think you can just walk away from your crimes? No, you can't." Xeno said playfully.

"Well, we're fucked." Emory scoffed, and a small tear rolled down her face.

"Like I said before, I will control you until you get the hang of it."

"Do we have to do this right now?" Melanie asked, she could slightly feel her heart beating in her chest.

"No, a random time in the next week that I will choose." He smiled as he slowly closed his eyes

"How will we know?" Emory asked. Melanie could tell that Emory did not like anything that Xeno was saying.

"Oh, you will know. It won't be hard at all to figure it out. Now go, that is all I had to tell you." Xeno's screen slowly faded into black.

"Shit," Emory whispered and slowly turned around to leave.

"You're just going to leave?" Melanie asked.

"Are we supposed to stay?" Emory replied coldly before putting on her mask and leaving.

Melanie could tell that Emory was upset, she understood why. Melanie felt her heart beating, half from sorrow for her friend, the other half from fear. Neither of them could kill, hell, they wouldn't even hurt someone accidentally without feeling bad for weeks. Melanie stood up and went back home through the portal. She saw the familiar walls of her room and the broken cup on the floor from earlier that morning. After taking off the mask and putting it back in the closet, she bent down and picked up the glass shards. Wait, where do you even throw glass? She asked herself before pulling out her phone, opening Google, and typing in the question.

Don't throw it in a normal trash can or recycling bin, throw it in a special container. She read in her mind. "Well shit," Melanie muttered.

It's fine. She thought as she picked up the glass and put it in a tiny plastic bag, being careful to not move her wrist in a circle like she always did to prevent anything from lifting off of the ground. If it wasn't a heat-of-the-moment decision, she knew she would have put it in the correct container, but it was getting late and she was too stressed and tired to care. After disposing of the plastic bag, she threw on a different pair of clothes and lay down on her bed. The sun had already gone down. Rolling over on her side and closing her eyes, intentions of falling asleep, she felt a tingling feeling all over her body.

Chapter 11

Melanie suddenly felt her eyes jolt open. She was still in her bed, but she was unable to move. All she could do was hear and see, nothing else. What the hell? She thought while her eyes darted around the room. Suddenly, she heard a light giggle, it sounded like the giggle of a child. The giggling quickly turned into loud crying, then screams of terror. With each second, it got louder and louder, more children joined in.

"Don't listen to him!"

"Don't listen to him!"

"Please, don't listen to him! He can't be trusted!"

"He's not what he tells you!"

"Don't trust him!"

"DON'T LISTEN TO HIM!"

The voices continued to scream, yelling at her. Melanie tried to move her fingers to snap out of it to no avail. For a moment, it felt like she couldn't breathe like the world was closing in on her. Then out of nowhere, she jolted up, now sitting in her bed. Birds were chirping outside of her window as if nothing had happened. Melanie sat up in her bed with a puzzled look on her face that was soon wiped away by her mom yelling from downstairs, "Come on!"

Melanie quickly rushed out of bed to start getting ready for school. "Coming!" she yelled back at her mom.

The next night, nothing happened.

"I'm telling you Em, it was some freaky shit." Melanie said.

"Or," Emory started, "you just had sleep paralysis." she pressed random buttons on her laptop, looking confused.

"I doubt it," Melanie replied. She then saw what Emory was doing. "What's wrong?" she asked.

"Nothing's working." Emory continued to press random buttons on her laptop's keyboard.

Melanie held out her hand to Emory, "Here, let me see."

Emory turned it around to show her. Melanie only looked at it for a few seconds before asking "How long has it been since you updated this thing?"

Emory seemed confused. "I don't know, maybe the beginning of freshman year?"

"No wonder this isn't working..." Melanie muttered to herself before finding a way to update the system. "There, just give it maybe an hour or so and it'll be working again." Melanie handed back Emory's laptop.

"Oh my god thanks, you're such a lifesaver." Emory smiled.

That day was Thursday, meaning they had to go to their school's weekly mass ceremony. Not a big deal, Melanie could zone out just long enough to get through it.

After walking over, Melanie and Emory sat down next to each other. Only two more years of this. Melanie thought to herself.

Fifteen minutes into it though, Melanie felt a familiar pain crawl up her arm. She looked at Emory and saw that in her face she could feel it too. "You go," Emory whispered.

"What? No, no way I'm going! You go!" Melanie whispered back. Suddenly, the pin got more unbearable, now up to both of their left elbows. "Fine, I'm going."

Melanie got up and walked over to Mrs J. "Can I go to the bathroom?" she asked.

Mrs. J. nodded in response.

Melanie quickly hurried off to the bathroom, when she opened the door she saw that there was nobody else in there, she let out a sigh of relief as she closed the door.

She quickly did the hand code to summon her mask. The second it appeared in her hands she put it on. No door. She quickly paced around the small space until she remembered how to make a portal door. Stumbling into the warehouse, she said, "I have at most seven minutes before I have to go back, please make this quick." She then took off the mask. As she did, she could feel the pain in her arm quickly retreat.

Xeno's screen flickered on, "Where's the other one?" He asked.

"We couldn't come at the same time, our teachers are super strict," Melanie explained.

"Fine, I'll get her at a different time. Let's make this quick."

"Wait, I have to kill someone, like-" she cut herself off and paused, "right now?"

"With my help, of course. You and I both know that you would get caught in ten seconds if I didn't help you."

Melanie couldn't deny that, she was insanely clumsy and not at all sneaky. "And your way of 'helping' is by controlling me?" She asked.

"Yes, of course it is." he answered, "Plus, it would be nice to get rid of some of my creations. It's getting too overpopulated for my liking." Xeno added on.

"Can we get this over with, please? I'm not trying to get in trouble." Melanie spoke in an urgent tone.

"Fine, fine, just pay very close attention." After Xeno said this, Melanie felt something in her mind changing, her vision slipping and getting blurry before going back to normal. Melanie was no longer in control of her body, she was just watching it do things as if she was watching a movie but if it was first person and through her own eyes. She couldn't move, blink, or even speak on her own. She could only hear and see. She felt herself start to panic, holy shit holy shit holy shit what the fuck is happening?! She thought to herself.

"Calm down. I am unable to think when I am hearing your thoughts." Xeno spoke through Melanie, the words coming out in Melanie's voice. "And if I am unable to think, then this whole thing will take a lot longer." he paced around Melanie's body before opening a portal. Melanie noticed that when she was seeing what Xeno was seeing, she could see the portal doors and secret openings that she would only be able to see with the mask on at all times.

After Xeno stepped out of the portal, Melanie saw that they were in an alleyway. She took note of the surroundings that she could see, two garbage cans, and graffiti on the walls, and it smelled awful. Some rats scurried across the ground.

From the buildings around the alleyway, Melanie could tell that they were in downtown Raleigh. Why are we here? She thought.

"There are many homeless people here, they're the perfect target because they all have had enough hardships to be a successful soul collection and don't have anyone who cares about them, if they go missing it doesn't matter," Xeno whispered.

Melanie watched as Xeno did a hand code with her hands that she had never seen before. A knife then appeared in Melanie's hand and Xeno started to walk Melanie's body to the trash cans. He proceeded to lift the lid to find a homeless man sleeping peacefully on the piles of trash. The man was using an empty bag as a blanket. Xeno used Melanie's body to climb into the trash can, still holding the knife. All Melanie wanted to do was scream and run away, to not have any part of this, but she couldn't do anything about it. Xeno then lifted the knife slightly and stabbed the sleeping man in the neck, Melanie saw that the man's breathing stopped instantly, he was dead. Blood dripped out of his neck and down on the trash around him.

"That's how you do it, simple as that." Melanie heard Xeno say through her voice.

Then, Melanie saw a bright glowing orb begin to float above the now-dead homeless man. She saw her hands go out to hold the orb, the orb then being sucked into her bracelet.

A few seconds later, Melanie was back in the warehouse, able to control her body again. "You may leave now, I hope you learned something." Xeno's screen faded to black again.

Melanie quickly put her mask back on and left, the portal taking her back to the bathroom. She looked at herself in the mirror, there was only a tiny bit of blood on her hand. The warmth of a tear rolled down her cheek before she walked to the sink to wash the blood off. With no other place to put her mask, she put it in her pocket and walked out to where her class was.

"So what happened?" Emory asked as they sat down at the lunch table.

Melanie looked up, "huh?" she asked.

"With Xeno?"

"Yeah. He controlled me to kill someone." Melanie said as she took a bite of her food.

She saw the way Emory froze up, "oh," Emory paused, "who was it?"

"Some poor homeless man," Melanie responded. "He said he was going to get to you at another time, I'd guess later tonight or close to that."

Emory did not respond, she just looked down at her food, only poking it slightly. Melanie looked at her, "Em, I know it's hard after what happened to your brother, but I'm sure it will all be okay."

"I know, I know," Emory said quietly.

Melanie felt the tension between them was thick. She felt bad for Emory but didn't know what to do to make her feel better. "Xeno showed me a new hand code." Melanie finally said.

"Really? What does it do?" Emory asked.

"I don't remember what the thing was exactly but it looked similar to the one we use to summon those masks, but it summoned a knife."

Emory's eyes widened, "Dead ass?" she asked.

"Oh, so dead ass," Melanie responded.

"What was it like to know, have Xeno controlling you?"

Melanie thought for a moment, "It was kind of like those movies where you're watching from the point of view of the character, through their eyes."

"That sounds scary."

"It was watching my body do things that I had no control over, but it makes me feel a little less guilty."

"What if someone finds out, Mel? What are we supposed to do then?" Emory asked out of nowhere.

"I don't think it will happen, but if it does we should just plead insanity so we only go to a hospital for a few years instead of jail for life."

"That's not how that works..." Emory trailed off.

"It's not? There goes my plan."

"No, you only get sent to a hospital until they think you're stable enough to stand trial."

"Damn, how'd you know that?"

"I've been doing my research after what happened to my brother."

Melanie still felt bad for Emory. "Didn't Xeno say that if anyone found out about this the 'world as we know it would end' or something like that?"

"He said something like that, he talks professionally and it freaks me out."

Melanie nodded as the lunch bell rang. "Fuck, do we have to go back to class so early?"

"It's 12:45, that's when we always end lunch," Emory said as she stood up from the table to put her tray away.

Her mind was blank as she walked into her room, unable to think or even feel anything at all.

Chapter 12

Weeks passed until the last day of school. Same as their freshman year, they sat in the same classroom as their homeroom all day and watched a boring movie, painfully waiting out the hours until they were free for the summer. Throughout the weeks, Melanie and Emory still ride their bikes together after school most days, and had learned a shit ton of hand codes, allowing them to do pretty much anything that they want, and killed some more random people. Some were specific targets given to them by Xeno, but most were anybody that Melanie and Emory wanted. Xeno had taught them that the more trauma and emotional baggage that a soul had, the more power and use it was to him. Melanie noticed that she was starting to go down a spiral of uncleanliness. She began to forget things that she never had before, now only brushing her teeth and taking showers when she felt the motivation to, the days between which got longer and longer. Before she had met Xeno, she would have never gone a day without brushing her teeth, or two days without a shower unless she felt gross. Now, she would go many days without doing either.

Ring ring

The final bell of their sophomore year, thank god this is over, Melanie thought to herself.

"How many SC's are we gonna have to do this summer?" Emory asked as they walked out of the building. SCs stood for soul collections, meaning how many people they would kill and collect their souls. Emory had gotten over her fear of blood and gore, or more used to the thought of death and killing, and she had also gotten over what had happened to her brother.

Melanie sighed, "If he gives us another one of those five-in-one-week things, I'm so dead." she flung her head down.

"Oh yeah for sure, I can not do that again. It's not like we aren't free, it's just that it's stressful." Emory said, looking down slightly looking down at Melanie.

"Are we even allowed to die?" Melanie asked as she walked forward to the exit of the school.

"We're human, we have to die at some point right?"

"Yeah, but we have a God in our minds. And if god can't die and he's in our minds, then our consciousness can't die, and if our consciousness can die, then our brains can't die, and if our brains can't die then our bodies can't die." Melanie said in one breath, struggling to regain it after speaking.

"Woah," Emory started, "I couldn't understand any of that so I'm just gonna tell you to stop worrying."

"Easy for you to say. You're not the one who's worrying."

"You've always worried about dying, probably even before we met"

"Is that a problem though?"

"No, it's not a problem. I just think that you should live life a little bit and not be worrying all the time." Emory finished speaking before walking out of the school doors for the final time to start summer. "See you later." Emory smiled as she walked to her car.

"See you later," Melanie said, slightly waving back at her before walking to her own mom's car as well.

The summer months passed fast, before she could even blink it was already July 28th, her Sixteenth birthday. She never gave a shit about her birthday and didn't understand why everyone cared about it. It was just another day on the calendar for her. Usually, she would spend it in her room or hanging out with Emory. This year, she stayed in her room. She was so tired from all of the tasks that she and Emory had been assigned from Xeno, she just wanted a day to relax. It was around noon when she felt those cursed cracks crawl up her arm. The entire summer so far, she and Emory had been doing random tasks for Xeno almost every day, whether it was just some brain-numbing lecturer, or five SC's expected to be done in a week.

The cracks continued to run up Melanie's arm, slightly stinging as they kept growing. She groaned and got out of bed. "Happy birthday to me I guess." she muttered before putting on her mask and going through one of the portals.

When she stepped out of the portal, she didn't see Emory. For another five minutes, she waited there, standing awkwardly until she saw her stumble through the portal. Even after being at the Warehouse so many times, something about it still made her uncomfortable. It's just the spiders and rats. She thought.

"Hey Mel, happy birthday!" Emory said excitedly, wrapping her arms around Melanie.

Melanie felt her lips turn up into a smile. "Thanks, Em, but I don't know why people get so worked up over it. It's just a day."

Emory pulled away from the hug, "So is Halloween, and you love that shit."

Melanie couldn't deny it, she had always loved Halloween. "So do you!" she said back.

"Finally, it took you two long enough." Melanie turned her head to see Xeno's screen now fully turned on.

"I've been here for at least six minutes," Melanie said.

"I do not like repeating myself." Xeno started, "Anyway, you've both been good with your assignments so far." He paused. "I need ten soul collections in the next week."

Melanie felt her eyes widen "Ten?!" She yelled. "How the fuck are we supposed to get ten soul collections in just one week?!"

"You'll find a way."

"That's one and a half people a day! We can't do that!"

"You're more than capable."

"How would you know?"

Xeno stared blankly at them. "Woah, it's like I'm the most powerful being in this universe!" He hissed, his voice making a slight glitching sound at the end, like a lost connection on a call.

Melanie flinched when she heard him yell, it wasn't often that Xeno got upset, but when he did, it always made her scared.

"Doesn't mean we are!" Emory yelled. "Ten in one week is way too hard."

"When you work with me, you will do as I say, understand?" Xeno's voice glitched again. "You both have the power and the capability to get this done by tomorrow, it's your mind that's holding you back."

What the hell does he mean by that? Melanie thought. Though, she didn't ask.

"Are we clear?" Xeno asked.

"Fine, yeah," Melanie said finally.

"Good, now go."

Melanie and Emory got up and left. Maybe they'd both find some motivation to get it done.

Chapter 13

Six days passed and nothing got done. Melanie and Emory were borderline serial killers at this point! While on her phone, trying to relax, she received an email.

Blank

Unknown sender:

Are you stupid or something? What the hell are you doing?

X

Melanie stared at the message, well shit, she thought. She tried to delete the email, which to her surprise, actually worked this time. Her phone then rang, it showed Emory's name on the screen. She picked it up.

"Hello?" Melanie asked, putting the phone on speaker

"Did you get that email too?" Emory's voice was filled with panic.

"Yeah, why?"

"We have to get that done," Emory said sternly

Melanie was taken aback, "No we don't. What's he gonna do?"

"Hurt us?"

"But not kill us."

Melanie heard Emory sighing on the other line of the phone. "If I do five, will you do five?"

"That does make it a tiny bit easier I guess.." Emory replied.

"Great." Melanie hung up the phone. She grabbed her mask, the smooth plastic rubbing against her fingertips. How could anyone do this willingly? She thought, thinking about all of the serial killers who were seriously fucked up in the head.

Kill, after kill, after kill, after kill, it all blurred together. Melanie felt as if her skin was being dyed from how much blood she had gotten on them in the recent months "See, was that so hard?" Xeno asked as Melanie lifted the dead souls to Xeno's circuits.

Yes. she wanted to say but held her tongue as she watched Emory do the same thing with the souls. Their glowing white color was as beautiful as the night sky. They lifted into the screen, quickly being absorbed. The souls of people they collected could only be seen by them if they had their masks on, and could be stored in their bracelets until they needed to take them out again to give to Xeno.

Melanie and Emory both had to admit that it didn't make any sense. Why them? Why did they have to kill people instead of Xeno taking the souls of people who had already died? Why would a god entrust two sixteen-year-old girls to do his dirty work? How did the masks and bracelets work? Was it magic? And if it was, how is it even possible?

Summer quickly ended, school was about to start again and Melanie was in for another year of hell, more fire this time, though. Ironic for a school that teaches its students about god.

"Two more years," Emory said

"What"

"Two more years until we're out of here?" she repeated.

Right, start of Junior year, right? Two more years. Two more years. She repeated to herself throughout the first few weeks of school. Two more years. She said to herself when someone would be a bitch to her. Two. More. Years. She caught herself saying it when she or Emory would sneak out of class when Xeno needed them.

Even though they had gone up a grade level, most of their classmates and teachers were still the same people they were in classes within the years prior. Melanie hated that, she hated seeing the people who made her life more of a hell-hole. She'd just have to manage, it's what her mother always told her. In her opinion, she may have not had the best mom, but she sure as hell did give some good advice. While sitting in math class on a warm September day, Melanie looked over to where Emory was and saw that she wasn't looking at the board. The fuck? Emory loves math. Melanie thought. What the hell is she looking at? Melanie tried to follow Emory's eyes with her own and saw that she was looking at Megan, the girl who "betrayed" them to be friends with Brittany. When Melanie looked at Megan, she saw that she was looking back at Emory as well, and she was smiling. Both of them were. Melanie turned back to the board, lancing at the two of them, periodically through the rest of the class. Every time she looked, they were still looking at each other. She even caught a few giggles between the two, and not judgemental giggles, genuine giggles.

After class, she walked to the cafeteria with Emory.

"So what's up with you and Megan? Are you two suddenly friends again or something?" Melanie asked, giving Emory the slightest side-eye.

"You could say that."

"Why? Since when?"

Melanie heard the annoyed tone in Emory's sigh. "Since she apologized for just leaving us for Brittany."

"When was this?"

"Right before school started. I was driving around trying to get some things for my parents"

A week ago? Why hadn't Melanie gotten an apology? She used to be Megan's friend too, right? And wait, Emory, driving? She remembered that Emory had always said she would never get her license, that she was too afraid of getting in a wreck. "Why didn't she apologize to me? Not like I care but I'm just curious. And since when can you drive?"

"She didn't? Hmm, weird. I'll talk to her about it." Emory sounded slightly confused.

"You didn't answer the driving part."

"Oh yeah, I know I always said I wouldn't learn because I was too scared, but my dad got his license suspended for speeding so I have to do a lot of the driving now."

"That makes sense."

They eventually sat down at their lunch table. Even when they were eating, Melanie noticed Emory and Megan catching glances and smiling at each other. The glances and smiles did not look like ones you would give to someone who you had just recently become friends with again.

She thought she had been close with Emory, she was always the first person she would go to if she needed help. They knew and understood each other more than anyone had in either of their lives. But since the crash, she had somehow gotten closer to her. It was probably from having to spend all of their free time together. They loved each other, platonically, of course. But everybody wanted to be alone sometimes. Neither of them minded it, it was better that they were together more times than they were apart, helped them work things out better if they had a disagreement, which had somehow gotten a little more frequent as of late, some just being stupid things that they would be able to make jokes out of. Others took a little longer to get over. Even then, they were rarely ever apart.

Melanie found it weird when Emory suddenly blew off hangouts because she was "too busy".

"You're never busy." Melanie would say in protest, holding her phone up to her ear. "Plus we have to talk about how we're going to get some of these SC's done."

"Can't it wait until Xeno needs us again?" Melanie could hear Emory impatiently tapping her fingers on a table.

"I mean I guess but–"

"Great! Talk to you later!" the phone quickly hung up.

Weird. She thought.

Weeks passed, and Melanie did get an apology from Megan, eventually, and a genuine one too. She thanked her and moved on, like she said, she didn't care. What she cared about was why Emory was spending so much time with Megan all of a sudden.

"Melanie!" Xeno screamed her name to get her attention. She looked up to see his atrocious two-dimensional face plastered on the screen.

"Huh?" she asked in confusion.

"You and Emory have been... on the rather spacier side of things lately. I'm going to find out why."

"Okay." Melanie shrugged. He may have had power over her, but not enough for her to give a shit about said power at the moment.

She heard Xeno sigh, "Is it something at your school?"

Melanie looked up again. "What are you, my mom? Why ask if you're just going to figure it out yourself."

"Because it tires me out to go through your mind, trying to sort out memories and when they happened."

"You're God, right?" she started, "figure it out."

"I don't like the way you are speaking to me." Melanie heard the glitching and low static hum at the back of his voice. She knew that if she didn't shut up now, it would get messy. Something she did not want one bit.

"Fine, fine. I'll shut up."

"Five soul collections by tomorrow." fuck.

"What?"

"You heard me, now go." fuck again.

She left with a groan, calling Emory when she sat down on her bed and threw the dark Jackelope mask into her closet."

"Hey, Mel, what's up?" she heard Emory ask. Melanie could also hear someone else on the other side of the line. The person said something along the lines of "Who are you on the phone with?"

"Hey, where are you?"

"Out, why?"

"Damn, what made you go out on a Friday night?."

"Boredom I guess. I'm also with Megan right now. You can come over if you want, we're at her house."

Megan. Of course, she was with Megan. That was who she heard a few seconds ago.

"You just said you were out."

"Yeah, out at Megan's house."

All Melanie did was muster out a groan.

"Something wrong?" Emory asked, her connection cutting out slightly.

"I'm just tired, and I have to do five SC's by tomorrow."

"Just come over, let's all three hang out!" Emory laughed slightly.

"No way, I'm not hanging out with Megan."

"Come on, she apologized."

"Still, just not tonight. I should be going to bed. I'll have to get up at two in the morning to find someone."

"Okay, stay safe when you go."

"Like Xeno would let us be able to get hurt."

Emory laughed, "Right, right. Talk to you later."

"Bye."

"Bye." Melanie hung up the phone, set an alarm, and lay in her bed for a while. What am I doing? She thought. Killing people for god... how did I let this happen? She could feel her body slowly drifting off to sleep, not bothering to change her clothes, she knew it would be too much work for her when she had to wake up again. At least the hoodie she was wearing was comfortable.

Melanie was abruptly woken up by her alarm, 2:00 AM, on the dot. She slipped into some shoes and grabbed her mask. "Heh, fuck me," she muttered to herself before putting her hood over her head.

She and Emory were running out of homeless people to kill, there were only so many on the streets of North Carolina, and if every homeless person mysteriously went missing, they would have more of a chance of being caught. Whether it be by police, the FBI, or someone she loved. She held out for as long as possible for more stereotypical targets, like people in dark alleys who were stupid enough to be there late at night, vloggers in the forest who were trying to hunt down "the moth man" or any urban legend that had gained popularity on social media. Emory suggested that they killed the rich people, but that would leave a much bigger impact.

When Melanie regained her vision after going through a portal, she was in the same alley where she killed a man a few weeks prior. She remembered the way he screamed and begged for mercy. His matted-down beard moved in one singular motion when he shook his head due to what was probably years of not being able to take care of himself properly. When Melanie remembered the way he begged, she laughed slightly. She would have slapped herself right then and there if she didn't find it funny. The alley connected two sidewalks, it was bare, other than the trash cans that businesses in the city used. The brick walls felt extremely rough, if she rubbed her hand any faster along its surface she would begin to bleed.

Cameras.

If there was one weakness to a killer's plan it was cameras.

She and Emory had learned a hand code that would turn off every camera within a 500-foot radius and erase the footage from the past hour. It was very helpful, more helpful than Melanie initially thought. When she remembered the cameras, she quickly moved her hands into the motion, she watched as the small red blinking lights went out. God, she was tired. The only way she remembered about the cameras was by hearing the beeping that she wouldn't have been able to hear without her mask.

Melanie paced back and forth in the alley, poking her head out periodically, mask and hood still on. Waiting for some poor soul to come into the alley so she could be one soul closer to being done for the night. It felt like she was waiting hours, she didn't bring her phone in case she accidentally called someone.

She waited.

And waited.

And waited some more.

That was until a woman turned down the alley. Her long platinum blonde hair was pulled back into a low ponytail. She was wearing a short dress that fit around her body nicely like she had been partying. She also seemed drunk. Very drunk, drink-away-your-problems drunk. Melanie ducked behind one of the dumpsters and watched as the woman stumbled her way through it. When she was where Melanie wanted her, she struck. She plunged her knife into the woman's abdomen with a sickening squish sound. The woman gasped in surprise for air, unable to scream or struggle from how drunk she was. She collapsed to the ground, her blood pooling around her. Its metallic smell filled the air. Melanie pulled the knife out of her body, more blood squirting out. She aimed for the heart next. Plunging the weapon deep into the woman's chest. How could someone lose this much blood and stay alive? The alcohol in the woman's system must have kept her calm and her body numb. Melanie saw her brown eyes begin to flutter. Slowly getting longer and longer between each one. They fluttered more and more until they eventually closed and never re-opened. Melanie took the knife out of her body when she saw her soul hovering over her body. She held her bracelet up to it and watched as it stored it until she needed to give it to Xeno, like a hen sitting on its egg before it hatched. "Holy shit," she said to herself.

That kill was different from every other one she did, this time, she enjoyed it. A breathy laugh left her mouth, one full of disbelief and enjoyment.

No. She shouldn't feel like this. Shouldn't she? She looked at her hands, seeing the woman's blood on them made her laugh again.

Stop it!" she told herself. Thinking like that didn't make her a psychopath, right? She's being forced to kill, of course, enjoying it doesn't make her a psychopath.

One down, four to go.

Melanie went all around the city trying to find unsuspecting victims, it wasn't until five in the morning that she finally collected the five souls she was assigned. She was tired.

"Xeno!" she yelled when she got to the warehouse. The mechanical hum of Xeno's digital form came to life, emitting a low buzz.

"Melanie Adelia," Xeno said her name in a disapproving tone. Melanie felt a chill run down her spine.

"Woah, okay, never call me by my full name again," Melanie responded while walking towards his screen. She had always been cranky when she was tired.

"It makes people afraid."

"Were you trying to scare me?"

"Not necessarily." Xeno laughed, his voice glitching as he did so.

"Freak..." she muttered under her breath.

"Excuse me?"

"Nothing, nothing." she winced as she gave the souls to Xeno.

Xeno simply let out a small hum, "You killed an alcoholic?"

"I killed whoever I happened to pass in alleys and on a Friday night, most of them are alcoholics. And don't you like the souls of people with 'sad backstories'?" she stepped away from Xeno's screen, doing air quotes with her fingers.

Xeno sighed, "You need to pay more attention to who you are killing and where you are killing them."

"I am!" Melanie protested.

"Really?" Xeno sounded jokingly skeptical. Acting like she did something wrong was something he was starting to do to make her and Emory pay attention to what they were doing. Melanie rolled her eyes, still covered by her mask, but did not answer.

After a few moments of silence, Melanie finally spoke, "Am I allowed to go home now?"

"Of course-"

Before Xeno finished speaking, Melanie had already gone through a portal to go home.

When she got home, she went to the bathroom to wash up. The blood she had on her began to crust on her skin and under her fingernails. Melanie couldn't take it. The sensation overwhelmed her. She turned on the shower and watched as the water ran for a moment to heat up before she stepped inside. The hot water was scolding her skin. The blood of those she killed slowly trickled off of her body and down the drain. She rubbed some shampoo between her hands before massaging her hair with it. Some blood came out from her hair, its color muted from being mixed with the water, leaving a mesmerizing swirl around the drain before being sucked into it.

Chapter 14

That Monday, they were in physics class when Emory slammed her head onto her table in physics. They had Ms. Lodge again for their junior year, and so did Brittany and Megan.

"I swear to god I'm going to piss on someone." Emory groaned.

Melanie's eyes bulged in surprise as her head slowly turned to face her friend. "Please don't."

"No, I will if this assignment doesn't start to make sense soon."

"Pissing on someone is the answer?"

"Yes!"

"Just use Google."

"Google's ass, I'd rather die than use it."

She rolled her eyes, "Just look at your notes then." Melanie looked up from her assignment to look at Emory. And of course, Emory was looking at Megan who was on the other side of the classroom from them. Next to her was Brittany, who was absently talking to Megan who was not paying the slightest bit of attention to her.

"You expected me to take notes?" Emory said as she looked away from Megan and back at Melanie.

In the halls, the only thing on the walls were posters for the upcoming spring dance. It was like Saint Cathrine's version of prom. They weren't allowed to call it that because the priest of the church considered the title of "prom" was "sexual" and that it "encouraged the youth to stray further from god." The posters in the halls were decorated with flowers, bees, and suns. Light colors scattered across the pages made by the school's media students. The media students were students who signed up for the yearbook club. The club was small, with only about ten people. All of them were freshmen who didn't know that "yearbook club" really meant sitting on your ass for an hour and waiting for the teacher to hopefully give you a useless assignment to pass the time.

No students were ever allowed to work on the yearbook, that's why so few people signed up for the club. False advertising.

It seemed like the same three posters were filling up every free inch of space on the walls, changing some parts of the usual blue walls to rectangles of either light pink, light yellow, or light green. It seemed as if everybody was seeing these posters for the first time based on the way they looked at them. Every time you entered the hallways, someone was always staring at it with their friends asking each other if they had a "date" for it. The dance was advertised as something for "just friends to go to" seeing as dating wasn't allowed publicly at school, but nobody was going to follow that rule. Why would they?

Melanie looked at one of the posters next to Emory. "How much do you want to bet that someone's gonna have a baby in the bathroom?" Emory asked, louder than Melanie had expected her to speak

"The fuck?"

"I said-"

"Yeah I heard what you said, I think this entire hallway heard what you said."

"So? You think it's gonna happen?"

"Definitely," Melanie hated to admit it but Emory was probably going to be right. "Everybody at this school is either a goodie goodie or a whore."

"So what are we?"

"A mix?" Melanie questioned jokingly, causing Emory to laugh.

The bell that signaled that they had one minute before their next class started rang. It confused many of the students because it had the same bell sound as the real bell. For a school as small as Saint Catherine's (student-wise and building-wise), the five-minute passing period was more than enough time to walk around the entire school more than twice and still get to class on time. Most of the students thought that the one-minute bells were not necessary and were more annoying than helpful. "Fuckkkkk," Melanie complained, "I don't wanna go to history."

"C'mon, I'm not getting another phone call home. My parents would kill me." Emory grabbed Melanie's arm. "I'll drag you if you don't come willingly."

Melanie let out a loud, dramatic groan, letting herself be dragged into the hallway.

Then she heard someone whisper her name. The voice was too familiar.

Melanie whipped her head around, and so did Emory.

"Did Xeno just say your name?" Emory asked.

Melanie rolled her eyes before turning her head back around and began walking, turning into their history classroom. "I don't know he's been making me do a lot more SCs lately and just overall pissing me off. How much has he made you do?"

"It's been a while since he's made me do one. Maybe a little over a week since my last one?"

"I would kill to have your workload right now."

"I'm busy with family stuff though!" Emory playfully shoved Melanie as they took their seats when the bell ran.

History class was one of the only classes that they had a new teacher in. He was about five-foot-six, and his straight hair was black, but his beard was the color of ginger hair. He always showed up to his work in a suit and dress pants, always covering the shirt with a jacket of a sports team that he liked. The sides of his beard were always freshly shaved. Just from his voice, anybody would be able to tell that he was a big history fanatic. "I'm just going to take attendance now," he said as he grabbed the same paper he had read off for attendance every day since the beginning of the year. "Melanie Adelia?"

"Here."

"Emory Brooke?"

"Here."

There was a name that nobody had heard before, "Larely... Marley? Am I saying that right? You're new here, right?"

Larley nodded before laughing, "Yep, I'm new." The girl had short curly brown hair, brown eyes, pale skin, pink glasses, and freckles. There was nothing very interesting about her.

"Well. Welcome to Saint Catherine's, Larley." he coughed before continuing. "Kyle Tinkson?"

"Here, Dr. C." Kyle jerked his head up and winked. It made Melanie want to vomit.

"Okay, Kyle. there was no need for that." Dr. C. rolled his eyes.

Kyle was the kind of guy who could make straight girls gay, and gay girls gayer. If you could even make someone turn gay.

After he had finished taking attendance, he got on with the lesson. Something about the American Revolution. Melanie almost fell asleep.

To stay awake, Melanie tried to let her mind wander. Think about random things to prevent her brain from letting her fall asleep. And she succeeded.

At home, Melanie scrolled through her phone to fight boredom.

Come over.

Why?

Please? :(

Ok, I'll be there in like 10 min.

Melanie grabbed her coat and rushed downstairs. "I'm going over to Em's house," she called out to her mom while putting her shoes on.

Her mom made an approving noise, quietly allowing her to go.

Her bike had sat on the side of the house, tethered down to the ground by a rope. It hadn't been touched since the crash, almost a year ago now. Even if it had been a while, the way to Emory's house was engraved into her brain. She couldn't forget it even if she had tried. The trees, the bumps in the road, even the sounds of the creek that ran through the backyards of many of the houses in their neighborhood, even the change in smells as she passed each house was the same as always. Most of the houses smelled like smoke though, either from a barbeque or a cigarette. When she got to Emory's house, she left her bike where she always had, and knocked on the door. Emory's mom answered with a smile.

"Hello, Melanie. Emory's just upstairs in her room." She greeted, stepping out of the way to allow Melanie to enter the house. Her red curls bounced as she moved, shutting the door for Melanie.

"Hey, Mrs. Brooke," Melanie replied before quickly making her way up the stairs. Melanie always thought Mrs. Brooke's posture was strange, she held her chest out way too high, it made her look like she was taking a big deep breath in and holding it everywhere she went.

When she went upstairs, she saw that Emory's door was open. Melanie knocked on her door, even if it was open to let Emory know she was coming in in case she was changing or doing something that someone would want privacy for. "Come in." she heard Emory call out loudly. She didn't know that her door was open.

"You didn't have to scream so loud." Melanie said, stepping into Emory's room.

"Shit was my door open?"

"Yeah."

Emory sighed, "Oh well."

"Why'd you ask me to come over?"

"We haven't hung out much after school, other than when we're doing stuff for Xeno, but I don't think that counts as "'hanging out'." she put air quotes around the words.

"It doesn't." Melanie crossed her arms over her chest jokingly.

"Which is why," Emory started, "I found something."

"Really? What?"

Emory grabbed her phone from beside her, pulling something up before handing the phone to her. "I found this just now when I called you."

Melanie looked at the screen, they were reports from the diary of a lesbian woman from the 16th century. The handwriting was close to illegible, like Melanie's, and the paper it was written on was old and wrinkled, even though it was clear that the person who was trying to salvage it tried their best to make it easy to read.

To whoever has found this, I am dead. I can not take the stress anymore. It is killing me inside and it has for years. I have had to carry the guilt of murder for years, ever since I was just fifteen years of age it was like it had become my life. I fear I have lost all feelings, feelings for my wife, feelings for my family, hell even feelings for my cat. I feel so empty now in a way that I have never felt before. The whole idea of a new life was so enticing, that I forgot that my actions have consequences. Now as I look back on it, oh, the things I would give to go back and do it all over once again. If I could, I would have broken his stupid bitch-faced mask the second I laid my hands on it. I wish I could have stopped him from doing this to anybody else as we had promised. But he told me that my soul would just get reused for him again like it always has. Xeno doesn't know the pain he's causing to us, to everyone around us. Our lives are not distractions! I didn't want to leave my wife alone with him, stuck being forced to do what he needs, but I need to get out of this before I run myself into the ground. I know she can stop him without me. I wouldn't have married her if I didn't. Love sometimes isn't shown physically, we will meet in another life. I love you, Amelia.

With love, Constance.

Melanie's mouth hung open. "Holy shit" she blinked a few times. "Did I read that right, did whoever this Constance woman is know Xeno?" She handed Emory's phone back to her after doing one last glance over the entry.

"That's what it said." Emory took the phone and tossed it to the edge of her bed.

"But she said that souls are reused. Our souls haven't been reused." Melanie reasoned.

"We don't know that. In retrospect, Xeno's been pretty secretive unless we ask. So I think-"

"Then why don't we ask?"

"I was just about to say that." Emory narrowed her eyes.

"Oh, sorry," Melanie said, laughing slightly. Emory laughed back.

Emory got up and pulled her mask out of her closet. Melanie used a hand code to make it appear. Emory turned back around, "Damn, I kinda forgot that we could do that."

"How did you forget?" Melanie asked, mask in hand as she stood up. "Xeno reminds us almost every time we see him that we have to use our hand codes to stay 'under the radar.'"

"He does?" Emory cocked her head to the left.

"I mean, he has been. He started it recently."

"I don't remember that."

"You've been zoning out whenever you're around him, no shit you don't remember." Melanie held back laughter when she spoke.

"It's not my fault that Megan's cute." Emory put her mask over her face.

"What?"

"What?" Emory responded as if she hadn't said anything in the first place. She quickly went through the portal in her room.

"Wait!" Melanie yelled before putting on her mask and following her.

The warehouse hadn't changed in the year they had been going there, yes they had put in things like lights to make it feel less dull, but other than that it hadn't changed. The occasional rat scurried through the place, but it was never a big problem. "Xenooo," Emory shouted, drowning out his name in a sing-songy voice.

Melanie went up behind her and playfully slapped her arm.

"Owww" Emory rubbed her arm.

Xeno's screen turned on. "What is it? You took time out of your day to come and talk to me when you could have just talked to me from the comfort of your own home. Would've been easier for both of us."

"Don't care, you wouldn't have responded anyway. We need to talk." Emory walked closer to the screen.

"About what?"

Emory took out her phone and pulled up the picture of the old diary entry. "Who's Constance?" she asked sternly.

Xeno looked to Emory, then to Melanie, and then back to Emory again. "Where did you find that?"

"There's like five articles about it, and it was found yester-day." Emory put her phone back in her pocket.

"Constance was one of my best workers, her wife too."

"That doesn't answer the question." Melanie butt in.

"You had other workers?" Emory questioned.

"You're right, it doesn't." Xeno sighed. "I'm guessing you know about your souls, correct?"

"As in?" Melanie twisted her hand up.

"As in they have been reused more times than I can count. You two were the first two souls I ever made. Almost every-one else is a copy or randomly generated. That's why I trust you to trust and follow me, then I do the same for you."

"So who was Constance?" Emory asked.

"Melanie was Constance, in one of the past lives. They share the same soul."

What the fuck. Melanie thought. "Excuse me?" she said out loud.

Xeno blinked twice, his red pupils seemed to flash like headlights on a dark road. "I find it easier every time I train you two again. Your minds and bodies don't remember what you've done, but your souls do. You also get more powerful in every lifetime." He chuckled.

Melanie's eyebrows creased, "you told me that souls get sent to some sort of 'trash file' before they get put into another body. Is that true for us?"

"It's a little different." his voice pitched up at the end of his sentence. "You two get more time if that makes sense."

"No, it doesn't. It really doesn't." Emory put her hands in the pockets of her pants.

"I spend more time on you working to mold you back into what I need you to be, to become stronger. At this rate," He laughed, "there will be a day where your souls are more powerful than I am, as long as you don't make the same horrible mistake Constance and Amelia did."

"Mistake?" Melanie asked.

"Constance killed herself, and Amelia found a way to shut me off. I was annoyed as hell after that happened."

"Shut you off?"

"They cut off my connection from this place. I'm not supposed to be here, and none of this is even supposed to exist. It all just happened by chance."

"So, how did you get turned back on?" Emory questioned.

"That was the only time I let your souls come back to earth with the knowledge of the life you once had, minus the part where they hated me. Didn't take long for them to help. I trust you won't make the same mistake that they did, right?" Xeno's tone began to get more bitter. His eyes squinted in thought.

What the hell? So technically they had been doing this since the beginning of the human race. Wonderful. And what did Xeno mean by 'it happened by chance? "We won't, I promise. So-" Melanie was cut off.

"That's enough questions for today." he said, voice filled with negativity.

"But-" Melanie was cut off again, by Emory this time.

"Okay!" Emory said, voice sharpening. "Mel, maybe we should just stop asking things for today." She whispered into Melanie's ear.

Melanie sighed, "fine." she muttered.

Xeno's mouth, or what seemed to be his mouth, curled into a smile. "I was going to wait until later to ask this of you, but I feel like it might be best that you start planning now, mentally and physically."

Both Melanie and Emory cocked their heads to the side in unison. "What does that mean?" Emory asked.

"Looking into your memories, I found some distractions." his voice glitched. And Emory's expression shifted to one more nervous than anything. "Brittany and Megan, who are they?"

"I hate them," Melanie said sternly.

"They're fine, Brittany's sort of a bitch but Megan's nice." Emory struggled as she tried to talk about Megan. She was acting strange, first saying Megan was cute before they left, now barely being able to speak when her name was brought up.

"To you, maybe." Melanie looked at Emory and rolled her eyes, shifting her weight to one of her legs.

"Well, whatever you think of them, they're becoming distractions. Both of you know this, right Emory?" Was Emory being targeted? Did they know something that Melanie didn't?

"I wouldn't say that..." Emory's voice trailed off.

Xeno hummed, "Right." He paused for a second. "You have that school dance coming up right?" he asked.

"In a month. Why?" Melanie shifted her weight to her other leg.

"Nobody expects to get killed at a school dance, they see it as a place of safety." Melanie couldn't argue, she would even feel safe at a school dance. Even with the low security that there was, everyone was so afraid of getting in trouble that they didn't dare to try anything.

"You're going to ask us to kill Brittany and Megan?" Melanie asked.

"Exactly!" Xeno exclaimed.

Melanie didn't think that they were that much of a distraction to have to kill them. It would be nice to have them out of her hair for good. When she looked at Emory, smiling, she had a different expression. She was tense as if she was about to cry. Her hands were shaking slightly. "You have until then to prepare, being killed there would add to their soul's power. Can you do that?"

Melanie nodded, but Emory stayed still. Emory then stood up, shakily, grabbed her mask, and walked back through the portal back to her house.

"Good," Xeno said before his screen went dark.

Melanie quickly followed behind her friend. "Em, wait!" she called out before appearing back in Emory's room. Emory had somehow looked even more frazzled than she looked a few seconds ago. She knew she wasn't okay, but she still had to ask. "Are you okay? You just ran out and you look..." Melanie was trying to find the right word, "terrible."

Emory turned around to face Melanie. "No, I'm not! Why would I be okay right now?!" She yelled, tears quickly welling up in her eyes.

"Why? It's just Brittany and Megan." Melanie had been starting to suspect something between Emory and Megan, but the way Emory was reacting had confirmed it.

"I don't give a shit about Brittany, she can die for all I care, but Megan doesn't deserve it!" Emory had started to change, just like Melanie. When Emory was younger, she didn't want anything more than for people to live, even people who had wronged her. Now, she didn't care unless they meant something huge to her.

"It's not like you're dating her or anything, right? Cmon, it's fine. One less person to make fun of us, well two."

Emory stayed quiet, her mouth opened as if she was about to say something, but no words came out for a while. "Well," she started, stopping as if to gather the courage to say what she was going to say.

Oh shit.

"Megan and I have been dating! For a long time. We kept it a secret because I knew you would flip out and Megan knew Brittany would freak out!" a tear rolled down Emory's face. Oh SHIT.

"Em, I... I didn't know. But it's not like you love her or anything, right?" Melanie felt like kicking herself for not realizing it sooner.

Emory didn't say anything. The tension was thick, it had never been like this before. "I can go if you want me to?" Melanie finally said.

"If you want to go, I just need a minute," Emory said, turning around to her mirror and wiping the tears off of her face.

Melanie took that as a sign to go. "I'm sorry, Em. I really am." She said before she left Emory's room and went downstairs to ride her bike home. She felt guilty the rest of the day, but she knew there wasn't anything she could do to stop it. She didn't know what she was supposed to feel.

Chapter 15

The morning of the dance had arrived. Melanie and Emory had been planning the kill, simple and easy. Step one, Emory would lure Megan to an empty room of the school that Melanie was already in, which Brittany would follow. Step two, turn off all of the cameras that were there, plus in the hallways on the way to the bathroom. They couldn't have anybody see them walking the halls with blood on their hands, step three, kill them, easy. Emory said she didn't want to look at Megan when she was in the room, it would be too much for her to handle. Understandable. Emory had warmed up to the fact of what they had to do, but it didn't mean she liked it. Who even would want to kill their lover? Melanie got to school a little earlier than Emory, which was very uncommon. They always either got there at the same time, or Emory got there first. Emory didn't even show up to class until one minute before the first period. Emory was off the entire day, making her vibe stick out from the other students. When everyone was talking and laughing about that night, Emory was dreading it. Melanie was dreading it for Emory. She didn't care about Brittany or Megan, but she did care about Emory.

"What if we just don't do it?" Emory asked as she looked at herself in the mirror of Melanie's room. The same mirror where Melanie had seen Xeno for the first time.

Melanie frowned. "We both know that the punishment for not doing what Xeno wants will be so much worse than heartbreak." Melanat looked to Emory, putting in the star earrings she wore almost every day. She went over and stood next to Emory in the mirror.

"God, what are we doing with our lives?" Emory asked, disappointed. The two of them felt the pain of the cracks crawling up their arms, though they stopped about two inches from where they had begun at the bracelet.

Melanie put her hand on her friend's shoulder. "I think that just answered your question."

Emory laughed, it was the first time Melanie had heard her laugh in the past month. It made her smile. Before leaving her room, Melanie quickly grabbed some lavender leaves. A scent to cover up any smell of foul play.

Emory's mom had driven to Melanie's house to pick the girls up. Melanie's mom would have taken them, but she had been out since she had gotten home from school. "Thanks, Mrs. Brooke," Melanie said as she got out of the car.

"No problem! You girls have fun. Text me when you want me to pick you up, okay Emory?"

Emory nodded and her mom drove off. They could hear the music coming from the gym even from outside. "Oh fuck I forgot the only thing they're gonna play is country music." Melanie rubbed a hand on her face as she walked in with

Emory close behind her. The sun was setting, crickets were chirping loudly outside.

Inside isn't great either, it was clear that the people who had put this together tried to make it what the kids would want, but they failed miserably. Everyone looked like straight people in a gay bar, not supposed to be there. They stood around, some had drinks in their hands, and others were standing and talking to their friends. Melanie saw Brittany and Megan almost the second she walked into the gym. "When should we do it?"

"Soon as possible, before anybody notices that they're here." That was going to be impossible, Brittany was popular, making everybody want to talk to her and be around her. Her snobby, stuck-up attitude made Melanie sick.

Thankfully for them, Megan didn't like the attention Brittany shooed everyone away, but only for a short time. Melanie sighed, seeing that now would be their only time to get them alone, "I'll go to the janitor's closet."

"Upstairs right?"

"Mhm."

The upstairs janitor's closet was big, had cleaning supplies to clean up any messes they made, was right across from the bathrooms, and best of all was secluded. Melanie didn't care how Emory got the two upstairs, she just had to do it soon. As she walked up the stairs, her legs felt heavy as if someone replaced her blood, muscles, and veins with cement. When she got to the janitor's closet and tried to open it, it was locked by a padlock that needed a four-digit code to be opened.

Fuck.

Melanie tried to think of a quick solution, trying every combination of numbers she could think of off the top of her head, some being the date the school was founded, hell she even tried the day of the bus crash. She then looked at her hands. Xeno had taught them two hand codes a few weeks ago, one to make fire, and another one to make sparks of electricity. The fire and sparks were both purple. She moved her hands in the pattern of the spark code, zapping the lock on the door, causing it to open and fall off.

She was getting impatient hiding in there until she heard voices talking from behind the door.

Step one was complete.

Melanie quickly shut off the cameras with her bracelet.

Step two was complete.

The closet door opened slightly more and Emory and Megan walked inside. Brittany was standing outside of the closet near the bathroom. "You're sure we won't get in trouble for this?" Megan asked Emory.

"Oh, I'm one hundred percent sure," Emory smirked, causing Megan to let out a laugh. Emory kissed Megan's cheek, causing Brittany's eyes to widen and she stepped into the closet angrily.

"What the fuck is this?" Brittany yelled, gesturing to Emory and Megan.

"Brittany, it's not what it looks like." Megan put her hands up slightly in defense.

"Then what is it?" Brittany scowled.

"We're dating. We have been for a little while." Emory said.

Melanie shifted between the shelves and the boxes. She didn't turn the light on to prevent them from being seen, which made it even harder to see Melanie and Emory due to them both wearing black. She shut the closet door, locking the four of them inside, in the dark. "What the hell is going on?" Brittany called out. God, her voice was annoying.

The thing about the fire was that it was used for light, not just for warmth and to cook food. She used the fire hand code, causing a small purple flame to appear about an inch above her hand. "Hello!" she said in a cheery voice, giving a half-assed wave with her free hand.

"What the fuck is that? Megan do something!" Brittany demanded, pointing to Melanie.

Megan stayed still, she clutched Emory's hand. Brittany seemed to think that this was all a joke, Megan, however, the fear in her eyes was apparent as if she was going to pass out at any second from it. "Even in death, you want her to be your scapegoat, huh?" Melanie said softly as if she wasn't levitating fire or about to pull out a knife.

Before Brittany could say anything else, Melanie plunged her knife into the side of her neck, blood splattered everywhere it could when she took the knife back out a few seconds later. She swirled the knife around in Brittany's flesh to cause more discomfort than she was already in. She deserved this, didn't she? The more she jabbed the knife in and out of Brittany's neck, the more blood splattered onto her face, the walls, Megan's back, and even Emory. Despite her rampage, Melanie could hear Emory telling Megan to not look at what was happening. "Hey, hey, Megan, just look at me, okay? Don't look at what's going on over there."

Her hands were coated with blood, it oozed down her arms like water as Brittany fell to the floor, gasping for air before her eyelids closed for the last time. When she turned to face Megan's back, her hands were being held by Emory as she told her to breathe. Melanie didn't think twice before she stabbed Megan in the neck as well. The neck was the quickest way to kill someone. She heard Megan gasp and Emory tried to grab her as she fell to the ground. This time, instead of moving the knife around inside her body, she simply stabbed her twice and let Emory hold her lover's dying body. The darkness of the room only being illuminated by the purple flame in Melanie's hand. "I'm sorry, I'm so sorry." Emory managed to get out of her mouth, tears flowing down her cheeks as a sob escaped her lips.

Melanie backed up, letting the two of them have their moment. She watched Emory hold Megan, one hand trying to plug up the stab wound, the other holding her head up. Her eyes flashed with something of regret. "Go get help!" Emory yelled, blinded by her emotions.

"Em..."

"GO GET HELP!" Emory screamed, louder this time.

"Emory you and I both know we can't!" Melanie yelled back.

Emory sobbed as she held Megan's body close to hers, hugging the now corpse. A soul floated up above her body as if beckoning for (or taunting) her to grab it. Emory reluctantly took the soul, storing it in her bracelet before gesturing to the soul floating above Brittany. "You gonna get that?"

Melanie quickly turned and took Brittany's soul in her bracelet.

Step three was complete.

There were a few minutes of silence interrupted by the occasional sniffle from Emory. "Shit what are we gonna do about the bodies?" Emory asked with tears in her eyes.

They hadn't thought about that. "Shit!" Melanie muttered aggravatedly. "First we have to clean up the blood." Melanie grabbed a box of wet wipes that were for some reason stored in the janitor's closet. Nothing abrasive to ruin the tiles, as if they were never there. "Maybe after we clean up this mess, we can bring the bodies to be burned somehow? You can keep some of Megan's ashes." Melanie was thinking off the top of her head, trying to come up with solutions to their mistake.

"I don't want her ashes, I want her back!"

"I know but-" Melanie was cut off.

"And where would we bring them, huh? It's like we can just drag them out through the front doors!"

"We can bring things through the portal. We'll take their bodies to the woods and start a little fire."

"Are you sure we can bring things through the portals? If you're lying we are both fucked!"

"Totally!" She lied. She had never brought anything other than herself through the portal. She hoped that it would work if they had held onto their bodies. "And after we do that, we can come back and pretend like this never happened." Melanie opened the box, grabbed two of the wipes and rubbed them onto the floor. The blood was quickly picked up, the metallic smell now mixed with what could have been a distant cousin of a flower.

The wipes were tainted with deep red blood that would make anyone freak out if they knew it was real. Putting on her mask, Melanie created and opened a portal behind the warehouse. She grabbed Brittany's body, Fuck please work. She said in her mind before stepping through the portal. Brittany's dead body followed. The gash in her neck began to turn a deeper crimson shade as the air from the outside world reacted with her blood that wasn't being circulated throughout her body anymore. Melanie did a silent cheer before she saw Emory step through the same portal, holding Megan's body. Emory had stopped crying slightly, but a tear did fall down her cheek every few minutes. They came quicker when she looked at Megan's body. "Told 'cha," Melanie said in a snarky tone, trying to lighten up the mood. Based on Emory's reaction, she could tell it was one hundred percent, not the time.

Melanie quickly gathered a bunch of sticks and placed them in a pile. She set them ablaze with a purple flame she created. The grass around the sticks burned as well. Piece by piece they dismantled Brittany and Megan's bodies and tossed them into the fire, their flesh melted away, then their muscles, until all that was left was their bones. Melanie grabbed some leaves, spit on them, and watched the fires calm themselves. "Em, go grab a shovel."

"You forgot to bring one?"

"No, there's some in the warehouse." Melanie had put them there a few days earlier.

Emory sighed. "Alright." She went around to where the overgrown glass doors were, opened them, and there the shovels were; in the main hallway of the building. Melanie and Emory had been through this hallway no more than three times in her life, but every time they saw it, it was like something was different about it. Emory grabbed the singular one that she could, the other one was covered with bugs.

Emory came back quickly to Melanie and handed her the shovel. "I could only grab one, the other was covered with bugs."

"Gross." Melanie shuddered before looking back down at what remained of what had been two living, breathing girls less than thirty minutes ago.

"You need help moving those...?" Emory questioned softly.

Melanie nodded before gathering about a quarter of the bones and carrying them to a nearby tree. She set them down and began to dig a hole deep enough to keep their bones in. The hole was not that big, only two feet deep, and two and a half feet wide. There was just enough space to store the bones. Melanie and Emory gathered the bones and put them into the hole as quickly as possible. Before they filled the hole back up with dirt, Melanie pulled out the lavender from her pocket. She put some over the bones, filled up the hole, and then put some more about an inch above surface level. "That should even out the smell." Melanie said as she dropped the shovel and wiped her hands together. When she was done, she picked up the shovel again and turned her head to Emory who was standing right beside her. Emory's brown hair seemed to turn black under the night sky, while on the other hand, Melanie's blond hair kept its look no matter what time of day it was. "Should we give their souls to Xeno?"

"That's a dumb question. Why did you ask that?" Emory fidgeted with her thumbs.

"You're right, my bad." she jokingly put her hands up. Of course they had to. That was one of the reasons why they had to kill them.

Time seemed to stop as they walked to the main room of the warehouse, taking the same path that they had taken to get to it after the bus crash. "It's like we've walked this so many times before," Melanie stated.

"We probably have, since y'know, the whole 'our souls being put into other bodies thing'."

Emory did have a point. If their souls did transfer over to other bodies when they died, then maybe they have explored every inch of that place. Megan Maybe they had once known it better than they had known themselves. That was probably a stretch, though. By the time they had walked through the hall and opened the door to the main room where Xeno was, he was already on. The two girls were silent as they gave Xeno the souls. It was like every other time before, but now different because they knew who the souls belonged to.

"Does it feel different?" He asked.

"Does what feel different?"

"Does killing feel different when you know the person you're killing?"

"Is it not supposed to?" Asked Melanie.

"It is supposed to feel different, it shows that you care about what we're trying to do."

If she cared as he said, she would do everything that Xeno said without question, and without feeling any guilt for it.

Chapter 16

Emory didn't show up to school the next Monday, or the days after. Emory rarely missed school, only if she was in the hospital did she not come. The news about Brittany and Megan made national headlines, but the police had no leads. Saint Catherine's however, thought that Megan and Brittany died because of being bullied which made them all have to sit in a gym for thirty minutes and discuss the negative effects of bullying. There was a big window in one of the hallways that looked down into the gym. If someone were to look through that window during one of those assemblies, they would say that everybody looked the same. A sea of blues and whites that blended into the walls. Exactly what the school had wanted. As the principal spoke about how "tragic it was to lose the girls," Melanie couldn't help but feel like a weight had been dropped on her shoulders.

Going home was one of the longest car rides ever, even if it was only five minutes. Melanie noticed that her mom was breathing heavier than usual, must be her old age finally catching up with her. She thought. As they pulled up to the driveway, her mom said, "Go and get the mail. I can't be bothered."

Melanie let out a groan and swung her backpack over her left arm, walking to the mailbox and opening it with her right hand. It was a rather windy day, her hair blew into her face. When she got inside and placed it on the kitchen counter, her eyes accidentally looked over the front of the top letter that was addressed to her mom. She saw the words "debt collection overdue." Melanie had not been downstairs for very long in the past few months; she had barely been home at all. Even when she was downstairs, she didn't care to see what her mom was doing. Now, she looked into the living room where her mom resided most of the time. She hadn't noticed how dark the room was before, her mom looked like a villain in a Disney movie who was about to turn around in a swivel chair and pet a cat. The kitchen and living room were two separate rooms of the house, the walls were different colors, the lights were controlled by a different switch, and the atmospheres were wildly different. "Mom?" she called out to the almost pitch-black living room. "There's a letter here, it seems important. Something about debt?" she tilted her head, looking at the letter again. Her mom groaned and lifted her arm from her chair, a signal for Melanie to bring the letter over. Melanie grabbed it off of the counter and brought it over to her mom. She took one last glance at the front of the envelope before handing it to her. When her mom read it, she cursed under her breath.

"Damn son of a bitch." she muttered quietly as she crumpled up the letter and threw it onto the floor beside her. There were other crumpled-up papers in a pile on the floor,

Melanie suspected they were all the same thing. "Don't worry about it, I'll figure something out."

"Right," Melanie said suspiciously. Her mom couldn't have been in debt, right? She worked when she had to and they seemed comfortable. And if she was in debt, who would she be in debt to? Her brain instantly told her that it was to a casino, but there were barely any casinos in the state. The second thing that came to her mind was that they hadn't paid the bills on time, but she knew that her mom had paid someone to do them.

"Melanie, I said don't worry about it." her mom said again.

"I wasn't!" Melanie protested.

"What did I say about lying?"

"I'm not lying." a lie.

"It's all over your face. Wash it off."

It wasn't right? She couldn't have been that good at reading expressions. Melanie subconsciously touched her face in response to her mom's words. Her skin felt oily and coarse. There were tiny bumps, she hadn't been taking care of herself.

Xeno hasn't spoken to Melanie or Emory since the night that they had killed Brittany and Megand and it started to creep Melanie out. He was never quiet for this long.

Melanie stood on Emory's front porch, waiting for somebody to answer. It was still pretty early in the day, three-thirty in the afternoon. To her surprise, Emory's mom answered. "Mrs. Brooke? I didn't think you'd be home." Melanie said, surprised.

Mrs. Brooke sighed, "I took a few days off of work after what happened, just to be home with Emory. She needs me here." Mrs. Brooke placed her hand on her hip.

"Can I talk to her?"

"Oh please do. I think it would be nice for her to see you. Have you two been texting?"

"Not really, I thought I would give her some space."

"That was probably for the best." Mrs. Brooke sighed once more, "Emory's upstairs in her room."

"Thanks!" Melanie said, rushing up to Emory's room.

Melanie knocked on the door. A broken voice came from inside, "Come in."

Holy shit, Emory did not sound good. If Emory laughed it would make things a little better right? Melanie opened the door and leaned on the doorframe, her arms crossed across her chest. "A whittle birdy told me that you could use some assistance," she said in a deep, babyish tone.

Emory let out a small chuckle as her mouth dropped in concern. She had her phone open to funny cat videos on YouTube, a coping mechanism that she had. There were tissues all over the floor of her bedroom. She was wearing a dark layered shirt with dark shorts, a much darker wardrobe than what she had previously worn before the incident. A pink, fuzzy blanket was wrapped around her body.

"Oh come on, where's the Midwest princess that I knew? Looks like she's doing a bit more falling than rising at the moment." Melanie commented, noticing her friend's change in appearance.

"She went over to MSI."

"MSI, seriously? If you're listening to MSI in 2025, you're either super old or super depressed."

"Can it not be both?"

Melanie laughed loudly, "Do you remember when we were 14, and you were super upset about failing one of your tests-"

Emory cut Melanie off abruptly, "Don't even start with that." Emory weakly lifted her finger to Melanie's face.

Melanie moved Emory's finger away, "and we went to karaoke and sang femininominon, and didn't notice that Kyle Tinkson was there."

"I hate that memory and I always will."

"No, you don't because you had fun. You just think that because that Kyle bitch was there."

"I did have fun I guess, where are you going with this? I swear to fuck if you drag me out to karaoke again-"

"No! Oh my God, I won't do that!" Melanie laughed. "Just remember how easy it is to feel better."

Emory groaned and curled up in her blanket once more, lying her head down on her pillow.

"There hasn't been a lot of school work since you've been out, just a lot of assemblies and shit."

"Fuck yes." Emory groaned again.

Melanie felt a strong urge to hug Emory, so she did. A long, tight one that Emory returned. "We are in this together, as much as we hate it or not. And unfortunately, it's not something we can get out of ever."

"You think if we write, 'annoy the fuck out of him' some-where on the entrance to the warehouse it will make our-selves in our next life piss him off just enough that he shuts himself off and just watches the human race burn from a distance?" It was clear to Melanie that just by the tone of Emory's voice she was feeling better.

You're saying you want us to annoy Xeno so much that he theoretically shoots himself?"

"Yes!"

"That sounds like a shitty plan."

"It could work!" Emory protested.

"Or it could get us shot."

"With what?"

"I could name many things."

Riding home, she felt a sense of dread. As if something bad had already happened.

When Melanie walked into the house, the sun had already set. It was around nine at night. She placed her shoes by the door and walked around the bottom floor of the house. She noticed that her mom had gone upstairs to sleep for once instead of downstairs on the couch. She looked over to the living room where her mom would usually be, only for her eyes to land on the pile of crumpled- up letters from earlier. Her mom seemed so secretive about them, way too secretive. Despite her better judgment, she had to check out what the deal was with the letters. If they weren't important, why not throw them out instead of letting them sit crumpled up on the floor? Melanie took a step forward towards the pile. The floorboards creaked under her weight as she walked. A light skim of one of the letters would hurt, right? She pulled one out of the pile that read, "Payment Due" on the front in big bold letters. No way. She thought as she turned it over. The envelope had already been ripped open but the paper was still inside. When she pulled it out, it felt like it had burned holes in it. She looked over at the front of the letter again, addressed to their house, but it was sent in 2006, two years before she was born. It was sent from California.

In 2010, when Melanie was two years old, her dad left in the middle of the night after getting into a very heated argument with her mom. She never knew her dad, what he used to do, what he looked like (her mom never showed her the pictures), or why he left. "He was a bad man." Her mom would say whenever she asked. "Never cared about either of us. Only about himself."

She pulled the paper out of the envelope, stop stalling. She told herself. She unfolded the paper, crinkled slightly from her mom trying to crumple the envelope. Skimming over the page, she saw the words; 'Lacie Ivory Adelia', her mom's name. '200,000 USD', 'debt', and 'prison'.

The wind blew against the house, causing it to creak loudly, startling Melanie. She dropped the letter back into the pile but didn't pick it back up again.

Two hundred thousand dollars was a lot of money. Did her mom owe that much? And to who?

Melanie stood up and took a step back, turned away, and didn't look at the pile again.

Chapter 17

"Who the hell wears white to commit murder?" Melanie asked on a video call with Emory.

"Obviously my dumb ass." She responded while putting one of her white shirts in the sink, soaking it with cold water, her phone propped up against the faucet. Melanie let out a light giggle. "Oh shut up, at least I finally got out of bed."

That was true, she wasn't wallowing in sorrow in her bed anymore. "That's like, the number one rule, Don'tdont wear white."

Emory groaned, "I know, I wasn't thinking." Emory opened the bathroom closet, causing a pile of clean towels to fall over onto her, messing up her hair. "Shit-" she exclaimed before bending over to pick them up. She sighed and grabbed a bottle of hydrogen peroxide.

"Why do you have so many towels?" Melanie asked

"I don't even know. It's like there has to be fifty towels in this closet at any given moment." Emory turned back around and put the hydrogen peroxide on the sink. "Oksy how long do I let this soak for?" Emory asked out loud, reaching for her phone and exiting the call app which put her on pause.

"Thirty minutes probably works." Melanie responded.

Emory's screen quickly went back to her face. "Thanks. I was just gonna search it up, though."

"You don't have to now." Melanie smirked.

They both sat in silence for a little while, until the buzz of the faucet came through the phone. "I swear, Mel, if I'm ever this stupid again, kill me." Emory said as she rolled up her sleeves and put the peroxide on her shirt.

"I would but," She paused, "I don't really wanna do all of those SC's all by myself."

Emory groaned and leaned down over the sink, water droplets coating her arms "You're so awesome." she said sarcastically.

Melanie smiled into the camera, "I know!"

Emory pulled her shirt out of the sink, "does this look clean enough?" The shirt looked fine, but before Melanie could see, quickly Emory hung it up on a drying rack, "Whatever, I'll just say it's ketchup."

SC's inside of a house was Emory's thing, also Emory's idea. Melanie had only ever done house SC's with Emory, never done one by herself. "I thought you said you weren't going to wear white again," Melanie said, looking at the white tank top and sweatpants that Emory was wearing. Melanie herself was wearing all black, better to blend in.

"It was all I had! And it's gray, thank you." Emory snapped back.

"A very light gray."

"Shut up!"

Melanie raised her hands in a way to say "Alright fine."

"This is the house right?"

"No, it's across the street." Melanie said sarcastically.

"Great, let's go!" Emory started to walk in the other direction.

Melanie grabbed Emory by the collar of her shirt before she could get too far away and pulled her back, "Nope, I was being sarcastic."

"Shit, my bad." Emory choked as she was pulled back.

"Dummy," Melanie grunted as she let Emory go. She lifted her left hand and circled it in a clockwise rotation in the air, the hand code to turn off cameras.

The two of them stood in the dark nighttime spring air, the smell of pollen pungent around them. The house they were looking at was very unkempt. Vines and greenery crawling up the siding. The shudders were falling off of the windows and dark stains plagued the edges. The back door was the closest entrance that they were facing, there was a beige curtain over it. There were curtains on every window. Every light in the house was out, it looked like nobody had touched it in years. "How do we get in?" Emory asked.

"The door." Melanie walked up to the door in front of her and turned the handle. Locked. "Not the door." Melanie frowned as she put her mask back over her face. "Portal time," she said in a sing-songy voice. Portals were made with intention and focus. Trying to make one was useless without it. Melanie mapped out the frame of a door with her hand, her eyebrows furrowed as she concentrated.

Once they got into the house, The first thing that hit Melanie was the smell. It was like a mix of mold and sewer water. Melanie also noticed how dark the house was. Yes, it was nighttime. But usually, houses had at least some sort of light inside them, even if it was tiny light, it was there. The walls were a very unfriendly white, and there were cracks in the ceiling. The house looked uninhabited. "What the fuck..." Emory whispered as she put her mask off to the side of her head. Melanie did the same.

Melanie pulled a pocket knife from her side pocket. The blade was slightly duller now than when she had found it because she had never learned how to sharpen it. "So where the hell is this guy?" Neither of them talked louder than a whisper.

"Why would you assume it's a guy?" Emory asked.

"I don't know!"

Emory gestured to the stairs, "It's like you've never done a SC inside of a house before."

Melanie felt her face heat up. "I have! Totally..." She lied.

"Okay, sure," Emory said, nodding her head and trying to hold back a chuckle.

The floorboards creaked under Melanie as she went up the stairs. It reminded her of her own house. The way the floor creaked, especially when she went to look at the weird envelope pile, probably shouldn't think about that... she thought to herself. She heard Emory creeping up the stairs behind her.

Upstairs, there were a lot of doors, each seemed to have more dents in them than the last. There was a blue night light that was plugged into an outlet in the hallway next to a door that had letters on it that were hard to make out in the darkness of the house. The mask created a purple haze over everything visible. The doors looked like a collection of purple squares, the lines of it seemed to glow. The squares, Melanie found out, were a sign that a material could be walked through. Usually, it appeared on doors, sometimes on random walls, windows, and curtains. Going through the doors would have been a more efficient way of getting the job done, but the last time that Melanie had tried it she had a headache for days. Melanie walked over to a small table with a picture on it, using the hand code for fire to create a tiny flame for light that floated a few centimeters above her palm. Illuminated under the purple flame's glow was a wedding picture of a young man who seemed to be in his twenties and a young woman who looked a bit older than him.

Melanie raised her eyebrows slightly. "We might be killing two people today, Em."

"What makes you say that?" Emory asked.

Melanie handed the picture to Emory. Emory set it back down softly. "Then maybe we should get to it faster." Emory turned around and started to turn the knobs of a bunch of doors, quietly in case anybody in the house was awake. Melanie turned and did the same. The door knobs were made out of thick plastic and were painted a deep black. The first door she opened was a closet, then the bathroom, and then right before she could open the next door, she heard Emory inhale sharply. "What's wrong?" Melanie asked, when she looked back she saw that Emory was standing in front of the door that had words on it that Melanie couldn't see because of how dark it was.

"They have a kid!" Emory whisper-screamed as she quickly but quietly shut the door. Emory quickly created a small flame that floated above her hand. It was clear that Emory noticed the words but also couldn't see them. "There's no way I'm making this kid an orphan. No fucking way..." her voice trailed off as she read the words on the door. It read, 'Megan' in big pink letter stickers. Emory paused and closed her palm to put the flame out.

Melanie took a step closer to Emory. "Em, you okay?"

Emory didn't say anything, but her body was shaking slightly. In one sharp movement, she turned around and ran down the stairs, trying to go out the way that they came, not caring how much noise she made.

"Emory!" Melanie called, putting a hand out to her, but just barely missing her.

Inside the room Melanie was in front of, there was the sound of stirring and then an annoyed groan. Shit. Melanie thought. Em can wait, she figured. She had never done a house SC before, but it had to have been easier than finding homeless people or drunks on the street at three in the morning. "I think someone's in the house." A high-pitched muffled voice came from the other side of the door.

"Stay here." A deeper voice replied.

Melanie backed away from the door just as a man opened it. His hair was messed up from sleep and he was wearing a loose-fitting tank top and shorts. His eyes had dark bags under them. He was also holding a gun. "What the fuck are you doing in my house?!" The man yelled loudly.

Melanie's eyes widened. She had never stared down the barrel of a gun. Her body froze with fear, unable to do anything. Thankfully the masked hid the terror on her face from the stranger. She was unable to close her eyes, even if it was just for a split second to blink. In her panic, she didn't notice the small glowing square that stayed around the barrel of the gun until it started flashing and the words "threat" were shown. The font of the words were very geometric, made with squares and lines.

The mask had never done anything like that before.

She only had one thought in her mind. Don't let him kill you. The thought didn't seem like her own, but it seemed close enough.

"Stupid bitch!" The man screamed before finally pulling the trigger, sending a loud boom through the quiet house.

Melanie felt her body tense and her arms went up in front of her face in defense as she sharply inhaled. Her hand wrapped tighter around the knife in her hand, almost enough to turn her knuckles white.

After a second, Melanie didn't feel any pain, just a tiny spark in her abdomen. Then nothing. Melanie slowly lowered her hands, not fully ready to process whether she had been shot or not.

As she looked down, there was no blood. There was only a tiny bullet at her feet. The mask had the same tiny square around the bullet as it did around the barrel of the gun. Now, it said "threat neutralized". "The hell...?" The man said slowly in a shaky voice as he lowered his gun.

Melanie was also confused. The bullet had been shot at her. How did it not go through her? She shook off her confusion and straightened her posture. "Did... did you just try to shoot me?" she asked quietly. The man stayed quiet, a look of fear in his eyes. Melanie repeated herself, "Did you just try to shoot me?" She spoke a little louder that time. The man stepped back a bit, and Melanie took a step forward. Her grip loosened slightly on the knife.

The man kept walking backward until he was backed up against a wall. The man's wife was curled up in the sheets of the bed with fear. Melanie put her hand on the man's shoulder. Staring him in the eyes as she plunged the knife into his chest, aiming for his heart. Once she felt as if she had gone deep enough, she pulled it out. Blood gushed out of his body, oozing down his shirt. Some of which getting on Melanie. Once she was sure that he wasn't going to get back up, Melanie sliced down his stomach, letting him bleed out a bit more before standing up and wiping some of the dark crimson blood onto her pants. "Oh my god! Gerald!" the wife yelled.

Melanie grabbed his now floating soul before her head snapped towards the woman. "Look lady, I don't want to do this," she spoke with a hint of sarcasm. Stop. she didn't want to do it.

"Liar!" The woman yelled in protest. Melanie stepped to her. The movement wasn't her own. "Oh my god, please! I have a child!" she screamed, trying to look Melanie in the eyes. Or rather, the jackalope's eyes.

"Like I care."

Why would she say that? She didn't mean that.

Melanie quickly sliced the knife against the woman's side, causing her to let out a blood-curdling scream. Melanie stabbed her again in the side of her neck.

"Mommy?" a weak, childish voice came from the doorway. The woman was holding her side, hunched over in pain, and swearing at Melanie. When the woman heard the kid's voice, she looked up at her.

"M...Megan... Megan, it's gonna be okay, go back to bed sweetie." the woman stuttered, her voice strained heavily. She coughed once and blood came out.

"Okay, Mommy. Goodnight!" The girl, Megan, sounded so innocent, not a care in the world. She didn't even question who Melanie was or why she was there.

The woman coughed once more before blacking out. Melanie felt little remorse as she took her soul as well. She walked out of the room and opened the door to the kid's room. Megan didn't look to be more than seven years old. Her room was light pink with blue curtains that hung from the only window in the far corner of the room. Megan sat up in her bed and blinked a few times at Melanie. "Who are you?" she asked.

"Doesn't matter." Said Melanie as she leaned on the wall across from the girl's bed and hid her knife behind her back.

"I want my mommy."

What the hell was he supposed to do about that? Bring her mom back from the dead? "She's far away, kid."

"How far? I wanna see her."

"I can help with that, I think."

"How?"

Melanie scoffed, "like this." She quickly raised the knife and stabbed Megan's upper torso, letting her bleed. Her cries and pleas for help were quick but short-lived. Blood soaked her bedsheets, seeping down into the mattress. She wanted to say she was sorry for having to do that, but was she? She knew it would have been right to feel sorry, to feel some kind of remorse for her actions. But she just didn't.

Melanie picked up Megan's soul before her now lifeless body and dragged it to her parent's bedroom where her mother and father lay dead as well. With her mask on, she made a portal back to the side of the warehouse. One by one she carried the bodies and laid them in a pile only to set them ablaze seconds later. Melanie noticed that the fire she created was strange, burning things at the speed she needed. A three-hour-long process was done fully in three minutes as if the fire could read her mind. Once there was nothing left but bones, Melanie dug up the area where they had dumped Brittany and Megan's bodies just a few weeks ago and put the family in. She sighed, going back through the portal to the house she was just at to see if Emory was still there.

As she stepped through, the musty smell from before was now mixed with the metallic smell of blood. "Em?" She called out, "You still here?"

Melanie walked through the house, calling out Emory's name. The last place that she could check was outside on the back patio, where they had started earlier that night. When she went up to the back door, she noticed that the door was unlocked. As she opened it, she saw Emory pacing back and forth on the patio.

"Holy shit," Melanie said, slowly shutting the door behind her as she stepped further outside.

Melanie's sudden presence made Emory stop moving entirely and turn around to look at her. "Why the fuck did her name have to be Megan?" Emory whined. Melanie wanted to laugh but she knew Emory was being serious.

"I thought you were over it," Melanie stated.

"She died in my arms, Mel." Emory crossed her arms over her body as if she was hugging herself. She looked down

"It would've hurt a lot less if you didn't hold her." Why did she say that?

Emory looked back up at Melanie, "What?"

Too late now, "I said, it would have hurt a lot less if you didn't hold her!"

"You're an asshole," Emory said bluntly.

"It's just a fact." Both of them looked at each other for a few seconds before Melanie continued. "I was horrified in there, Y'know. I stared down a gun while being yelled at by a guy.

"He should've put a bullet through you," Emory muttered, just quiet enough for Melanie not to hear it.

"What was that?"

"He should've put a bullet through you. And you think I wasn't horrified there either?" Emory repeated, louder this time.

"Oh, because the kid's name was Megan?"

"Yes, but she was just a kid! And, and killing a family-"

Melanie cut Emory off, "Is what? Bad? No shit!" Melanie shot her arms out to her sides.

"It's immoral!" Emory yelled.

"Our morals are to just do what we're told without question."

"Do you not see how wrong this is?"

No, she didn't. She thought of a time that she might have. "It might be wrong but Xeno might kill us if we don't listen to him."

"He's not gonna kill us, just make our arms hurt."

"You don't know that."

"You don't know that he will, either." Emory spat. "And who knows, maybe we'll get killed doing one of these stupid soul collections! Then we'll never have to figure out if he would kill us or not."

"I got a little close to that tonight."

"What?"

"That guy had a gun."

"Was it loaded?" Emory asked.

Should it really matter, though? "Yeah. he tried to shoot me in the stomach." Melanie pointed to her abdomen right where the man tried to shoot her.

"What do you mean by 'tried'?"

"When he did, the bullet hit me, but it fell to the ground instead of making a mess of my organs."

Emory looked confused, "how is that possible?" she spoke with a lot of breath as if to catch it.

"Had to have had something to do with the mask." Ah yes, the horrible mask that Melanie had learned to enjoy the feeling of wearing. For her own sanity. "Before he shot me, when I was wearing the mask right?" Emory nodded, curiously. "There was this little purple square," Melanie made a square with her fingers, "that was around the barrel of the gun. The word threat was below it. When he shot me, the bullet just fell to the ground and the square disappeared and the words threat neutralized were around another square around the bullet."

Emory's eyes flickered back and forth between Melanie and the house that was next to them. "And the kid?"

"Megan?"

Emory froze slightly, but less than she would've early in the evening, "is she," she paused, "okay?"

"Her bones are with the other Megan." Just then, Emory went pale as if she was going to be sick.

Chapter 18

"Mel, are you crazy? Somebody's going to find them!" Emory said as she paced around the spot where the bones were buried. It was slightly more obvious now than before due to the mass of three more skeletons beneath.

"What are we supposed to do? It's the only thing that I could think of."

"Dump them in a river maybe?"

"There's no body of water anywhere near here, Em."

"Actually," Emory pointed somewhere in the distance, "just beyond those trees, there's a creek."

"How do you know that?"

"Research. Don't you do any?"

Melanie felt slightly offended. She did, just not on where to dump bones that didn't live inside human flesh. "Yeah, but, not on that."

It had gotten late, really late.

"If you want," Emory started, "you can go give the souls to Xeno, and I can go take the bones, all of them, to that creek and we can go home and sleep."

Melanie was surprised that she was willing to get rid of anything that reminded her of Megan Lawley. It was as if something had changed in her. "That works, I guess."

"I'll go get a shovel," Emory said, walking towards the warehouse's front door. Melanie followed suit.

In the front room of the warehouse, Melanie watched as Emory grabbed a shovel and a red barrel that was lightly stained with mud. Emory gave a half wave as she left to dump the bones in the creek.

The warehouse seemed to get creepier every time Melanie stepped foot in there, especially at night. There were a few spiderwebs that she had never seen before, probably new. She opened the cracking glass door, some of the already broken glass falling out of its frame as she opened it. A piece of it fell next to her calf, slightly scraping it. She kept walking. Just as she was about to call out for Xeno, his screen turned on.

"It's almost four in the morning."

Melanie scoffed, "So? We got what you needed. Emory's just getting rid of some evidence." she held the souls up to the screen, watching them as Xeno absorbed them.

He hummed in satisfaction before his eyes darkened, "You almost died tonight. Did you not?" Melanie froze as she put her arms down. "I watch every move that you two make, Melanie. Well, not at the same time, of course. But, answer the question."

To Melanie, it felt invasive that someone was watching her every move at all times. It seemed inhuman to her. She felt as if her privacy had been invaded. Nevertheless, she composed herself enough to answer his question. "Yes, that's what happened."

"If my memory is correct, he tried to shoot you and yelled 'stupid bitch' as he pulled the trigger." he let out a laugh as he said the last few words, slowly turning into a noise that would scare even war survivors.

"How?" Melanie asked bluntly.

Xeno stopped laughing, "How what?"

"How did I survive? How did that bullet not go through my body? I should be dead right now but I'm not."

"It's simple," Xeno said, "it's all about intention like I've said to you before. I saw you standing there, unable to move so I quickly snuck into your mind and told you to stay alive. Thankfully, he was half asleep and his intention to kill you was less than yours to live.."

Intention? What did he mean by that? All Melanie did when she was staring at the barrel of the gun was think about not dying, and she didn't consider that as having an intention for anything. "And what about that weird square around the barrel of the gun? The one that said 'threat'?"

"It's the mask's little way of telling you to get out of unsafe situations. It'll usually only show when someone's holding a weapon at you, or threatening to harm you in some way. It also lets me know what's happening just in case you two are too stupid to do anything about it."

Melanie tried to speak but no words came out. "And you think to tell me this now? Why do you always wait to tell us things until we almost die because we don't know them."

"It builds character." Xeno protested.

"How many times have you fucking done this with us? It has to be at least over one thousand times by now." Melanie knew that it was best not to yell at Xeno, it would just end badly no matter if she was right or wrong. It was the only thing she had to say so maybe he wouldn't take it as harshly.

"Watch how you speak to me, Melanie."

Melanie's face twitched as she tried to find the words to say, "I- uhm" she started.

"Don't start arguments that you know you can't finish," he spoke slowly. "Go home, you have school in the morning, correct?"

Shit, she forgot that it was a school night. "Fine," said Melanie as she put the mask back on over her head and went through a portal to go home.

She didn't notice the dried blood on her hands until she was already under her blankets. Whatever, she'll just clean it in the morning.

Melanie's eyes opened slowly, finding it hard to adjust to the light. Her phone alarm blared in her ears. "Ugh..." she groaned as she slowly rolled out of her covers.

She quickly inspected herself in her mirror. Crusted blood between her fingers, none in her hair (thank god), dirt on her arms and clothes. She thought about what Xeno had said, it's all about intention. How did she let herself get like this? Before this whole thing happened she would never have left dried blood anywhere on her, not even if it was for a slight second. Now, she was letting dried blood and dirt all over her body for hours on end. She chuckled at the thought of it before she let out a dramatic sigh before changing into her school uniform. She quickly headed to the bathroom to wash her hands and arms. There was nothing that could help the bags under her eyes, though. She'd manage. She knew she would have to if she liked it or not. Walking downstairs, she almost fell asleep, tumbling over but catching herself before landing on her face. She put some of the things she took out over the past few days back into her backpack and called out for her mom. "Mom, I'm ready!" she screamed, hoping to get her mom's attention.

"Emory's taking you today." Her mom said from the chair that she usually sat in.

Melanie jumped, not expecting her mother to be so close. "Why's that?" Melanie asked.

"Because I'm tired and I said so. They're going to be here any minute so go wait outside."

Melanie sighed dramatically again but obliged, slinging one of her backpack straps over her shoulder and walking towards the front door. Just as she opened the door and stepped out slightly, Emory's mom was pulling up outside of Melanie's house. The car's sunroof opened and Emory stuck her torso out of it. "Get in here bitch!" she yelled in a tone that was way too much for Melanie, no matter how much sleep she got.

Melanie simply chuckled, closed the front door, and walked towards the car as Emory lowered herself back into the passenger seat of the car. "Thanks for taking me, Mrs. Brooke," Melanie said as she opened the car door and sat down.

"No problem sweetie. Your mom's a very busy woman."

Busy? What did she mean by busy? All her mom did all day was sit in that damn chair and watch TV. Did it have something to do with those letters? Was her mom finally trying to pay off whatever strange debt that she had? She couldn't be, even a mouse would know that her mom was still too lazy to do that. Lost in thought, Melanie found herself biting on her nails. She was so out of it that when they arrived at school, Emory had to slap her slightly to get her to come with her. Melanie thanked Mrs. Brooke once again before getting out.

"Holy shit you look like death," Emory said when she got a good look at Melanie. "How long did Xeno talk to you?"

Melanie chucked as she tried to wipe the sleepiness away from her eyes. "Not long, but we were out super late."

"That's true."

As they walked to their classroom, Melanie didn't say much, she had other, more important things on her mind. It's all about intention. The thought came to her very intrusively. Melanie jerked her head up.

Emory laughed, "Okay, jumpy."

"How are you not tired?" Melanie asked.

"I am, but trying to be energetic kind of gives me some energy, you know?" Emory shrugged.

Sitting down in their seats, Melanie sat her head down. They were usually the first ones to homeroom, so she tried to savor the quiet before she would be drowned in screams for the next seven hours. "Emory, again, we're so happy you're back." Mrs. J. said.

"Thanks," Emory responded nervously.

"Oh and, this is for you." Said Mrs. J. as she handed Emory an envelope. "Mrs. Lawley requested that it be delivered to you specifically."

Emory took it, Mrs. J. walked away, and Melanie turned her head to face Emory, still laying it in her arms. Melanie could see the words "In remembrance of" in a curly font before Emory stuffed it in her backpack. Emory sat at her desk for a moment before getting up and asking to go to the bathroom. Melanie noticed the nervous look on Emory's face as she walked out.

Melanie thought it was weird that, especially in high school, you had to ask to go to the bathroom. Melanie waited for Emory to get back as more people funneled into the room.

Then more people.

Then more people.

Then soon their entire class was there.

Emory didn't come back until five minutes before the first period of the day. When she walked back into the classroom, she had a more dull look on her face than the nervous one that she left with. Emory sat back down in her seat, slouching slightly with her head resting in one of her hands. "Remind me to never run out on missions ever again." She said through gritted teeth.

Melanie brought her head up, rubbing the side of her face that had been touching the desk. Xeno must have asked to talk to Emory after she ran out of the SC last night. "I thought that was a given, but what did he say to you?"

Emory leaned back and tossed her arms to her side. "Literally nothing! He just yelled at me for running out and now I have to deal with those stupid crack things all day." She rubbed her head with her right hand, the one which didn't have the bracelet on it. "But I guess I didn't die so I won that bet."

Melanie knew it was coming, "There never was a bet."

"We should've made a bet."

"Oh yeah and if you died, who would've paid me?"

"Nobody, but you'd get to keep my bones." Emory smiled through the visible pan she was feeling in her arm.

"Who's to say I wouldn't throw your bones in that creek?" Melanie asked as the first-period bell rang.

"Touche," Emory said as she grabbed her bag with her stronger hand.

Throughout the day, Mealanie's mind kept going back to what Xeno said.

It's all about intention.

It's all about intention.

It's. All. About. Intention.

It started to take up her every waking thought. She never thought that four words (especially from a stupid jackalope) would affect her this much.

Every step she took, it's all about intention.

Every breath that she breathed, it's all about intention.

Intention.

Intention.

Intention.

"Get out of my head!" she groaned, pounding her fist against her head. The action warranted stares from a few of their classmates. Some with a look of disgust, some with a look of worry. More had a look of disgust, though.

No matter what she tried, she couldn't get those stupid words out of her head. Her hands suddenly started to feel extremely heavy and shaky. She had to lightly pat her hands on her lap to keep from screaming. The words seemed to circle her brain, weaving their way in and out through the folds and wrinkles of it. She wanted to take a pair of scissors and cut the words out of her, letter by letter. And to add insult to injury, every time she heard it it was in Xeno's voice. Occasionally she would hear him laugh and she eventually couldn't tell if he was there or if he wasn't. Her mind felt as if it was being punched every time the words were repeated.

The last time her hands felt heavy and shaky was when she had a meltdown in the school bathroom with purple electricity. The feeling grew up her arms and down her body until she started to spark. She got it to stop last time by calming down, but calming down isn't as easy when the problem is your mind. Melanie tried to focus on her breathing.

In and out.

In and out.

In and out.

It's all about intention.

It's all about intention.

It's all about intention.

Fuck.

The purple electricity, again.

No matter how pissed off it made her when it happened, Melanie had to admit it was beautiful in a strange way, it was like lightning but without the loud crash of thunder. It hurt like hell whenever it happened, and it was possible that it would hurt others. "Yo," Kyle started, "what the heck is going on with Melanie's arms."

Melanie suddenly remembered that she was in public. She looked over to Emory seeing that she remembered too. Emory tried to put a hand on Melanie's shoulder, "Calm down, Mel." she whispered.

"Can't you see I'm fucking trying?" Melanie whispered back, annoyed with Emory's statement and angry at what was happening to her.

Her breathing got faster and faster, making the electricity spark brighter and more frequent. Being in public didn't help either. The looks of all of their classmates just staring at her alone made her want to throw up, but now paired with this, she wanted to die. If everything that Xeno was saying about intention was true, it wasn't. Melanie never would have intended for something like that to happen ever, especially after the first time.

Emory quickly lifted her hand as she felt herself get shocked by Melanie. "Mel, look at me!" Emory yelled, shaking the pain off of her hand.

The electricity was bad. It hurt worse than any crack ever could. To Melanie, it felt like she was being burned from the inside out.

Calm down.

All that she had to do was calm down.

Shit, it shouldn't be this hard.

She reminded herself to focus on her breathing, to focus on anything other than intentions. It took a while for the sparks to go down, but even longer for the class to stop staring. Everybody's heads were turned to face Melanie and Emory, whose hand was on her shoulder. Whispers waved through the classroom. A few students said they were demons or witches, but neither was true. Melanie tried to stand to run, but she heard Xeno speak. "Raise two fingers on your left arm next to your head."

Melanie did as she was told, blindly.

"Move your fingers counterclockwise. It will erase their memory however long you need."

Again, Melanie did as she was told. The words flashed through her mind again, making her body feel hot with annoyance, but she decided to try and embrace it rather than fear it.

With what quite literally was a flick of her wrist; everybody had forgotten why they were looking at her. Their eyes went from a look of fear and disdain to confusion and blankness.

"Next time," Xeno started, "don't take all of the things I say and tell you this seriously. Everything that I do is to simply push you in the right direction."

Melanie sat back down in her seat and tried to push through the rest of the day, scared that someone would remember what had happened.

Chapter 19

The last week of school meant a week of testing. Which, of course, Melanie didn't study for. Every class had the words Finals Today on the boards.

Their school did final tests differently, the test would have as many questions as there were units in the class, and each question would be one thing from each unit. The school did it this way so students would have to study everything over again. Effective, but not ethical.

During their math final, their teacher came up to them and whispered to them, "I'm going to need you two to take those bracelets off." she said. She was looking down at their wrists.

She was talking about the purple bracelets that they had gotten from Xeno. "Sorry, but we physically can't take these off." Emory whispered back.

"And why is that?"

Emory tried to make up a lie on the spot, "Permanent bracelets?"

"Permanent bracelets, huh?" Both Melanie and Emory nodded. "I guess I'll just have to write the two of you up for dress code infractions then. You better find a way to fix it by next school year."

The two of them nodded before she walked away.

They got out of the class, and they both looked at each other, "One, we never learned half of that. Two, how does she expect us to get rid of 'permanent bracelets'? They're called permanent for a reason."

"She can't expect us to get rid of them if they aren't permanent bracelets. I'm happy she just wrote us up instead of forcing us to take them off or sending us to the office."

"That would suck, especially since our final grades would end up being such shit with zero on a test as important as that."

"One more year, just one more year until we can finally leave this hell."

"Melanie I swear to God if you don't shut up, I'm going to rip your teeth out." Something with her mom's voice said. The "thing" had her mom's body, but the face was blurred and jumbled.

"I didn't even say anything." she heard her voice say from the same creature.

It had been a while since she remembered a dream that she had, she still hated them just as much. "Just shut up, shut the fuck up." the creature spoke as her mom again.

She suddenly felt herself falling and felt a thick liquid stream down her cheeks, some of which got in her mouth.

Blood.

There was blood coming out of her eyes.

Through the streams of blood, she saw envelopes around her, the ones her mom kept in a pile in the corner of the living room. They fell with her and the curled edges and opening flapped in the wind.

She woke up right as she hit the ground.

Her bones cracked as she sat up in her bed and she put a hand around the front of her neck, the sheets were covered in sweat. Part of her wanted to go back to bed, and another part of her wanted to cry. She wouldn't normally care what her dreams had meant, but something about this one was different. Instead of crying, screaming, or falling back asleep, Melanie grabbed her phone.

Why did I have a dream about falling?

Feeling helpless.

She already knew why she dreamed about the envelopes.

Why did I have a dream about blood?

Guilt.

Guilt? She didn't feel any form of guilt, right? She thought she shouldn't. She didn't even have anything to be guilty of.

Maybe she did, just a little bit.

It was only the start of summer, the heat of the mid-year months still hadn't fully settled in and the long periods of rain still hadn't left and the trees still smelled like the leaves had just been given new life.

God, did Melanie want to be a leaf. Given a new life in the safe spot every time she burned out and withered away. To be given a new life, a rebirth after fucking everything up.

"I'm just saying, this place needs some air freshener," Emory said, moving her hand around the air of the warehouse.

Melanie grabbed Emory's hand and put it down. "You're going to blow the two of us up if you keep moving your hand around all willy-nilly."

"Willy-nilly?" Emory laughed. "I doubt randomly moving my hand is going to be a hand code."

"I wouldn't be surprised if it was." Melanie spoke with dramatic facial movements.

"Both of you, shut up." Xeno groaned.

Right, there was a reason they were there.

"Melanie," Xeno started, "That dream you had a few nights ago."

Fuck. "You know about that?"

"You're afraid of your mother, aren't you?" he asked.

Melanie wasn't afraid of her mother, she was just confused. "No, I'm just confused." she responded.

"You're afraid of what you might find out when you're not confused anymore."

"No-"

"You'll find out more if she's dead."

He's not implying that they killed Melanie's mom, right?

"You know you could... kill her."

"I'm not doing that." she cut in.

"Why not? You'll get answers sooner if you do. Those envelopes you found won't give you much. The only way you'll know the full story is when she's dead."

"I could just ask her!" Melanie protested.

"You won't do that, she won't give you an answer. She'll just tell you to shut up again."

He had a point, there was no way that her mom would tell her anything, not if she asked. Melanie looked at Emory, whose mouth was dramatically wide open.

"And it's not like she's doing anything for you. She does the bare minimum if I'm not mistaken."

At least she was trying, at least that's what Melanie thought she was doing. Her mom sent her to a nice school, drove her there (sometimes), and cooked for her (sometimes). Melanie tried to think of a time when she had thought her mom cared about her, but only one thought came to mind. The night that her father left the two of them, the night of the fight.

Her mom held her through the night, crying, telling her that everything was going to be okay. She remembered feeling her mother's tears fall against her thin hair at the time. The smell of tears was strong that night, enough to make the house smell like salty water for weeks.

Melanie didn't remember it much, since she was so young, but she knew that her mom cared about her, even if it was just a little tiny bit.

"She's doing what she can!" Melanie protested, instinctively taking a step forward.

"Is she?" Xeno chuckled. "I think all three of us agree that she would be better six feet under, her soul back in my possession, and to make things easier, I won't even make you bring me her soul. Just let it rot there, it'll find its way back to me eventually."

"Don't you need souls, though? Isn't that the whole reason we 'work' for you?" Emory chimed in, moving her hands to make air quotes when she said 'work'.

"A soul like Melanie's mother's would set me back centuries. None of us want that." he grinned.

Melanie wanted to know what her mom was hiding from her, but not bad enough to kill her. "If her soul will just make it back to you either way, wouldn't it be better to let her die of natural causes, you know, not have 'killed by own daughter' on her gravestone?" Melanie tried to argue.

"Come up with a fake death for her, perhaps. There are many ways a person can die in a house."

"But-" She tried to speak but her throat suddenly closed up.

"What did I say about starting arguments that you know you can not finish? You will do as I say, is that clear."

Melanie nodded as quickly as she could, she felt her throat open back up. She gasped for air. Emory grabbed Melanie's shoulder, Emory's hands were freezing. "I'm going to assume you want this done sooner rather than later?" Emory turned to ask Xeno.

"Not necessarily. Take as much time as you need, but do not mess it up." he grunted as his screen turned off.

Holy shit, she had to kill her mom.

"I'm leaving," Melanie said as she turned around.

"Wait, Mel." Emory grabbed onto Melanie's arm.

"What," Melanie looked up, her throat felt like it was being stabbed with barbed wire.

"I can help you if you want me to."

Melanie scoffed, "Oh yeah? And what would you do? Stand there and tell me that everything is going to be okay?"

"What? No! It's just that if you need help planning it out, I can help."

"No, Em. I can do it myself." Melanie sighed.

"Too bad, I'm helping anyway." Emory was always trying to help people. Maybe trying to help Melanie was her way of taking her mind off of being a murderer.

Maybe Emory felt guilty.

Melanie knew that she shouldn't argue with what Emory wanted to do, she was stern with the decisions that she made.

"Fine," Melanie said as she put her mask back on and went through the portal back home. She wanted to sleep but was scared that if she did, then she would have another dream or nightmare.

Chapter 20

It was now weeks into summer. Even just stepping outside felt like you were stepping into the third ring of hell. It was the fourth of July to be exact. The one day a year where Americans can set off fireworks without their neighbors thinking that they're weird. Emory had once compared Melanie to a dog because of how much the sound of fireworks bothered her. She was sitting at her desk, spinning around slightly in her chair as the first sliver of sun disappeared under the horizon. Even though it was barely dark out, the symphony of loud bangs and colors had started a long time ago. The desk in her room was messier than she had remembered, she never remembered a time when she had let multiple papers and pencils sit out the way they were now. Melanie never found the time to clean the mess up. 'Least painful ways to kill a person with a knife.' She searched up. If anybody saw it and questioned her, she would say it was for a project she was working on. That would divert any follow-up questions. The only things that showed up were help hotlines.

She searched up instead, 'Where is the least painful place to get stabbed?'

The hand and stomach fat would be the most effective, she found out. Both places can cause a person to bleed out, but there was enough muscle (at least in the stomach) for it to hurt a little less. The ear would be her next option, cutting it off would cause a person to bleed out, but it would also hurt like a bitch. Melanie rubbed the skin above her eyebrows. She knew that this would be hard, but she had to do it. As much as she hated it, Xeno was right. If she wants answers, it would be easier to just kill her. Besides, it was starting to become all that she knew how to do.

Melanie pulled out a tiny piece of paper and a pen. The only other murder that she had planned out was when she killed Brittany and Megan. Every other time she just went out and got what she needed to get done, done with nothing more than a get-in and get-out mentality. 'Is it more or less painful to get stabbed when you're asleep?' The internet told her that it was less painful.

Step 1 - Wait for mom to fall asleep

Step 2 - Stab mom when she was asleep

Step 3 - Get rid of the evidence and lie about her death

Step 4 - Burn the house down?

She crossed off the last step, she would be too scared and it would make things too obvious. How should her mom die? Well, how should Melanie say that she died? She weighed the options. If she said that her mom started choking, an autopsy would easily prove that she was lying. If she said that her mom had a stroke, then there would be the same problem with it not showing up on the autopsy. She pulled out her phone and texted Emory.

Come over

Sure

Thx

Emory knocked on Melanie's bedroom door. "Open up."

Melanie opened the door, "Thanks for coming, but you could have used the mask teleport thing to get here."

"Yeah, but you never do it."

"Because your mom would be suspicious if I just randomly showed up inside of your house. How did you get my mom to let you in?"

"Your mom loves me, Mel." Emory started, "So why'd you ask me to come over here?"

Melanie handed the paper to Emory. "I started to make a little bit of a plan."

"So you did." Emory took the paper and looked over it. "What's the one that's crossed out?"

Melanie sighed, "Burn the house down," she laughed, "I crossed it out because it would raise way too much suspi-cion."

"No shit it would." Emory handed the paper back to Melanie. "If someone were to ask 'Oh, how did the fire start?' What are we supposed to say? Yeah, we were only trying to get rid of the evidence after killing someone. We would go to jail."

"That's what I was thinking as I crossed it out."

"So when are we doing this thing? If we're doing it tonight I'm cool with that."

Melanie paused, "I," she paused slightly, "I need more time."

"That's understandable. And when your mom is gone, you can move in with me, okay? That way you won't have to worry about getting sent to an orphanage."

Melanie laughed, "Right because watching your mom drink wine while she's on the phone with her sisters and your dad is swooning over her is one hundred percent the life that I want."

"That was one time, let it go!" Emory softly shouted.

The first time Melanie went over to Emory's house, Emory's mom was drinking wine the whole time on the phone with her sisters while her dad watched sitting next to his wife. As a curious kid, Melanie asked why Emory's mom seemed so happy. It was a lot different from the sight she had at home. She wondered why her family looked so different from the one Emory had. At the time, Emory had a father, a mother, and an older brother, and her younger brother was still alive. Emory just told her that that's how her life looked and that she couldn't picture it any differently. "Totally a one-time thing." Melanie raised an eyebrow.

"It was!" Emory laughed before doing something between a scoff and a laugh, "I find that it's a miracle that we haven't been caught yet."

Melanie nodded as she grabbed her phone. She tried to click on the weather app but accidentally opened the news app.

Melanie was horrified to see a news report entitled; 'Raleigh, North Carolina homeless population down 75% in the past year.' her eyes widened and her jaw dropped slightly.

Emory saw the fear on Melanie's face, "What is it?"

Melanie quickly searched up how many homeless people lived in Raleigh. The average of all of the answers was well over one thousand.

All of the killings that the two had done had blended together in her mind, but she never expected the number to be that high.

"We've killed over nine hundred people." Melanie blurted out, her voice shaky.

"What do you mean?" Emory grabbed Melanie's phone and had the same reaction that Melanie did. "Holy shit, no, no I doubt that's right. A bunch of them had to die from diseases and stuff, too. Not just from us."

Nine hundred people. It was so much more than Melanie thought. It was much more than she had remembered. That number of dead souls was unfathomable. With that number of homeless people gone so suddenly, the police were definitely on Melanie and Emory's ass.

Melanie opened Google and typed 'Xeno' into the search bar. Only one search result came up. It was a Reddit thread from a week after the bus crash under "r/urbanledgends" titled 'COTJ IS REAL?!' The user's name was 'G0LD3N_BL00M' and the first words under the title were 'I live in Raleigh, and there was just a bus crash that was on the news very briefly. Only TWO people on that ENTIRE bus did not pass out! It doesn't make any sense and I'm pretty sure that the two people who didn't pass out were both fifteen! I'll update soon if they release any more information!'

Another post from four months ago was under it, 'Okay guys, I think I'm going to stop talking about this. I keep having nightmares and I have a gut feeling that I should just shut up about whatever the COTJ is. I doubt it's real anyway.'

What the fuck. "Do we have a fanbase?" Melanie asked, handing her phone to Emory.

Emory took a second to read it, her eyebrows furrowed. "Don't think so. They don't know any names, just the same curse thing that Mrs. Lodge told us about after the crash." She handed the phone back to Melanie.

"We should figure out who this is." Melanie said.

"How do you expect us to do that? Become hackers?"

Melanie smiled as if she had an idea.

"No, Melanie we are not-" Emory started to speak before Melanie cut her off.

"But, if we did, then we could find out so many different things." Melanie leaned back in her chair. "So if Xeno won't tell us anything, we can figure it out ourselves."

"That'll never work and you know it."

"Xeno's main form of communication is technology, right? What if we hacked into him?"

"Do you hear how insane you sound?" Emory asked.

"You want to know too!" Melanie tried to protest.

"Maybe a little, but it's not worth dedicating our life over."

"But Xeno is worth dedicating our lives over?" Melanie smiled and Emory's eyes closed slightly.

"I guess it is sort of a good idea, we could keep it in mind."

"If we do it would be so much fun, I heard it pays well too." No, she didn't, she didn't know one thing about hacking, how people become one, or what being a hacker as a full-time job even meant.

"I already said it was a good idea." Emory put both of her hands up to about the height of her ears, about two inches from the side of her head.

"Great!" Melanie had never convinced Emory of something. Especially because she had thought that when Emory said no the first time it meant that she wasn't going to change her mind.

Emory quickly changed the subject to get the two of them back onto the topic they were discussing before. "What if we," she moved her thumb across her neck, "your mom on the twenty-eighth."

"My birthday?" another firework went off, closer to the house, causing her to jump. Emory didn't acknowledge it.

"Yeah, well, it gives you time and you already said that you don't like your birthday."

"So your solution is to make it worse?"

"It's not going to get better if we're being honest."

Melanie couldn't argue. It would be better to make the hatred grow than try to fix it. "That could work."

"And," Emory strung the word out, "it will remove some suspicion because what teenager would kill their mother on their birthday?"

"We'll figure it out like we always do, right?"

"Exactly."

The sun had only gone down the tiniest bit more by the time Emory had left and the fireworks got a little more frequent.

The days leading up to the planned killing didn't feel any different from any other day. It wasn't until her birthday when she was in Emory's room holding her knife that she realized what she was about to do. "You ready?" Emory asked.

"Fuck, yeah I guess." Melanie was looking down at the carpeted floor. The entire day she had been lying down in bed, sleeping and dreading what was about to happen. "Em?"

"Yeah?"

"How much did it hurt when we killed Megan?"

"A lot, but that's because I knew that she also loved me. Mel, your mom doesn't show shit about how much or how little she cares about you. When she's gone, nothing is going to feel too different, trust me." Emory tried to sound comforting, but Melanie didn't think that it was working.

Melanie didn't want to believe it. There was a difference between the death of someone's mother and someone's girlfriend. She knew that she had to do it, as much as she didn't want to. "I hope you're right, Em," Melanie responded anyway.

"Do you have any idea what your mom is doing right now?"

"Probably sleeping." She just wanted to get it over with.

"Do you think we should go now?"

"That's probably for the best before I start feeling more guilty than I do right now."

"Right, let's get this shit done." Emory said as she put on her mask. Melanie did the same.

Melanie opened the door to her room and began to walk down the stairs, they didn't squeak as much as they normally did that night, or she just couldn't hear it over the beating of her heart that was now filling her ears. She let her thoughts consume her as she stepped up to her mom's chair, who was, as Melanie predicted, sleeping. "Go on," Melanie said, "Let's get this over with."

"Why don't you do it then?" Melanie looked from her mom's sleeping face to Emory's masked one.

"It's your mom."

"It was your girlfriend!" They were both whispering, "Sorry, too far."

"Damn right, it was." Emory crossed her arms and leaned herself against a wall.

Melanie raised the knife and lowered it again. "Just do it." She whispered to herself.

"Oh my god, just give me the knife" Emory walked up and took the knife from Melanie. Melanie took a step back, stumbling onto the couch.

She watched Emory raise the knife and stab her mom in the stomach, pulling it out seconds later. The sound it made was unbearable. It was hundreds of times louder than any of the killings that she had ever done before. The knife going into the flesh sounded like twelve ripe tomatoes being squished, she could even swear she heard something crunch alongside the horrible sound of a stab. "See how easy that was?" Emory turned around to look at Melanie.

Melanie couldn't move, as if she was paralyzed. She looked off to the side, at a random spot on the living room wall trying to not focus on her mother bleeding out. As much as she tried to not look, she still saw a large pool of blood that pooled on the carpet, staining it as it leaked more and more and the deep red puddle got larger and larger. Emory must have hit a vein when she stabbed her. "Not as easy as it was for you." Melanie was finally able to speak.

"Now we both know what it feels like to lose someone we love."

It was at that moment that Melanie remembered that she forgot to tell her mom that she loved her before going over to Emory's house. "Losing your girlfriend is a lot different than me losing my mom you know."

"Not really," Emory interjected, "especially with how different both of them treated us."

Melanie stared back at Emory "What the hell does that mean?" she asked

"You know, maybe it was easier for you to kill Megan because you didn't like her, and it was easier for me to kill your mom because I didn't like her."

Melanie finally stood up. She didn't know why Emory was acting like this. Emory did have a point though, but it didn't give her the right to say something as hurtful as that, especially in a situation that was as intense as that. "Even if that's true, why say it?"

"Am I not supposed to?" Emory's voice was cold as she stepped away from the body and set the knife down on the coffee table.

"Em, you're not acting normal. Stop being weird"

"You aren't either, you normally are thrilled to kill someone" she spoke sarcastically. "Can we just get her body out of here?"

"Not until we know she's fully unconscious." Even though her mom was fast asleep when she was stabbed, that doesn't mean she hadn't woken up slightly when the knife punctured her stomach.

"She was sleeping when I stabbed her and has been bleeding for the past five minutes. If she wasn't unconscious before, she's far out of it by now, especially with how much blood she's lost."

The wind howled outside of the house which caused it to creak slightly. Drops of rain began to hit the roof of the house. Emory walked behind the chair and picked up one of the crumpled-up letters. "What are you doing?" Asked Melanie.

"What are these?" Emory asked, turning the one she had in her hand over and trying to flatten it to read the few words that were on the envelopes.

Shit, "Letters from the government to my mom. I was worried about what they meant."

"So Xeno thought that killing your mom was the solution to helping you find out what these letters meant."

"I guess. Can you just put it down?"

"There are hundreds of these all in this small pile," Emory bent down and grabbed one of the papers off the floor that was out of an envelope, "Damn your mom owes a lot of money." Emory dropped the paper, letting it fall slowly to the ground. The pool of blood had already spread to the papers and when Emory let the one she was holding fall, some blood got on that one too.

Emory folded her arms over the back of the chair, watching Melanie's mom intently. The chair that was once a dark tan color was now a deep crimson from the blood stains. "I think she's out," Emory announced before turning to Melanie. "So are you going to help me or what?"

"You agreed to help me, not the other way around. I got it." Melanie stepped towards Emory and shooed her away from her. "Are we just going to do the same thing we always do?"

"Was that the plan?" Emory asked, Melanie hadn't noticed the blood on Emory's forearms until just then.

Melanie nodded and picked up her now almost-dead mother. It was true that it did hurt as she watched her mom get stabbed, but not as much as she thought it would. Even though it didn't hurt, she wanted to get rid of her mother from her existence. As if the short walk from the living room to the kitchen made her rethink everything she had thought about in the past ten minutes when she walked down the stairs. She walked into the kitchen because it was where the backdoor was, but before Melanie could open the back door, she set her mom down on the tile floor. She looked at the oven and turned it on before doing the hand code to start a fire. The purple flame levitated gracefully as it always did above her hand.

Just because she had crossed it out of the plan paper didn't mean that she couldn't do it.

"What are you doing?" Emory asked, stepping into the kitchen.

"Getting rid of the evidence." She said, walking over to a bottle of hand sanitizer. She opened the pump lid and poured some of it onto the kitchen counter. Get rid of the evidence, get rid of the memories, get rid of all of it. She thought to herself as she gently set the flame down onto the hand sanitizer. A giant flame erupted, the color of the sanitizer slightly canceled out the purple color of the flame she used.

If the police asked, then she would just say that when the fire started, there were some of those colorful fire packets lying around near it.

Since she had spread the sanitizer all over the counter, the fire had quickly spread more, catching a roll of paper towels on fire in the process.

The fire quickly surrounded the two of them, igniting every flammable thing, soon enough reaching the rest of the house. Melanie didn't move from where she was standing, she didn't even register how much fire there was until Emory opened the door to the back of the house and threw Melanie and herself out of it. The grass was wet as raindrops drizzled down, covering every inch of what used to be dry land. As she hit the ground, her mask fell off of her head. She picked it back up as Emory took hers off. "Put your mask in my bag," she said. Melanie did as she was told.

Melanie turned around to face the now almost fully blazing house, and her eyes widened.

"What have I done?"

Chapter 21

"What have I done?" Melanie asked herself.

"What didn't you do?" Emory asked, her voice trembled as well as her hands as she took her phone out of her pocket and dialed 911.

"Who are you calling?" Melanie asked, breathless.

"A fire station, duh!" She said as she put the phone up to her ear.

She tried to grab the phone out of Emory's hands as she heard the ringing start. "What are we going to do about my mom's body?" Melanie asked.

"Nothing, we just have to hope that the autopsy of her body doesn't show that she was stabbed." That would never work, and both of them knew it. If anybody had any sort of brain, they would take one look at the body and instantly know that she was murdered. The ringing on the phone stopped and someone answered. Emory tried to make herself sound more scared than she was while telling the person on the other end of the line the situation, the address, and how they 'didn't know what to do and panicked.'

Emory started walking to the front of the house, calling Melanie to follow with her hand while still on the phone.

"Yes, we're walking to the front of the house now." Emory responded to the person on the other line. Emory went on mute before stopping, "Mel, we have to get our story straight if they question us. There's no way we can tell the truth about what happened tonight."

Melanie nodded, "What if we say we were hanging out at your house, came over here, and when mom was cooking in the kitchen, had a heart attack, stabbed herself with a knife, and then the house caught on fire because we couldn't hear anything."

"That works for me." Emory responded, turned around, and started to walk to the front of the house again as she unmutted the person on the phone.

It wasn't long for fire trucks and the police to get there. They could tell how close they were to the house by the sound of the sirens. Watching the lights of the cars and trucks shimmer across the wet street seemed surreal. There were a bunch of neighbors standing outside, watching Melanie's house burn down. The night was hot enough that many people came outside in tank tops and shorts, some children came out and were just as intrigued by the fire as moths to a light bulb. The police tried to keep Melanie and Emory calm but also asked them some questions. "How did the fire start?" a policeman asked.

"The oven, I think," Emory responded.

"Where is the woman who is still in there?"

"In the kitchen."

"Why is the fire," he paused for a second to take a look at the burning house, "slightly purple?"

Crap, "There were those colorful fire tablets in the kitchen." Melanie chimed in, "My dad and I used to use them for campfires, but when he left we never finished the packs off fully." none of that was true, but she would just have to go with it.

"We're going to take you girls down to the station for some more questioning, you're not in trouble, though, okay?" Said an officer as he unlocked his police car.

They were so screwed. "Yes, officer," Emory said quietly, opening the door and getting into the car. Melanie did the same thing. The car smelled musty, it reminded Melanie of the car that she and Emory were put in after the bus crash sophomore year. The day that their lives changed, the day that if it had not happened, they wouldn't be where they were now.

As the car drove off, Melanie watched her mom be pulled out of the burning house by some firemen and then strapped onto a gurney.

As they turned out of the neighborhood, Melanie stopped looking out of the window and down to the floor of the car. There were at least five small empty water bottles on the ground. She looked over to the side that Emory was sitting on and there were even more over there. At each light that the car stopped at, Melanie kept feeling more and more anxious. Each turn they took, each breath that they cop made felt as if it made time slow down. She wanted to cry, to tell someone, anyone, the truth about what had happened that night, but she knew better, she knew that if she told someone, she would be in jail for the rest of her life. Even if they knew she was forced to murder The raindrops raced on the windows, some of them combining, causing them to go faster. Melanie and Emory didn't say a word to each other the entire drive. They both just sat in their seats, trying not to think about the mess that Melanie had caused.

The car pulled into the police station. "Alright, girls, get out." The policeman said as he parked.

Once inside the building, the two girls were led back into a questioning room. Melanie was instructed to wait outside while they questioned Emory first. A police officer was standing on the other side of the room to make sure that Melanie didn't try to leave. Why would she? If she did, that would just make her look more suspicious.

It took tenish minutes for Emory to come back out. Her head was hung low and she was looking at the ground. Emory sat down in the seat that was next to Melanie's before another officer came out and told Melanie to come with him.

Inside the room, there was a wooden table, two grey metal foldable chairs, and one fluorescent ceiling light that seemed as blinding as the sun. A window with brown rectangular curtains let a tiny bit of sunlight in, but not as much as they should have, seeing as the sun was already about halfway down at that point.

The officer who led Melanie into the room sat down and motioned for Melanie to sit across from him. The chair was uncomfortable and cold. He grabbed a notebook and pen from off the floor and set it on the table in front of him. "Hello, my name is Officer Ackerman. Let's start with something easy," the officer started, "what's your full name and date of birth?" The man seemed to be pretty young, he had short brown hair and stubble on his chin. He didn't look older than twenty-five.

"My name's Melanie Rose Adelia, I was born on July twenty-eighth, two-thousand eight."

The officer frowned, "I'm sorry you had to go through this on your birthday, Melanie. And at seventeen, this must be so hard for you."

Melanie didn't say anything, instead, she nodded. She would get through it, she had to.

"Can you walk me through what you did today? From when you woke up to just now."

Remember the story you and Emory made up. She reminded herself. "I woke up around ten and lay in bed for a while. Emory asked me to come over later in the evening on short notice so I did. When I got there, I left something at my house so I asked if we could walk there to grab it. When we did, we went up to my room. We ended up talking there for a while and then the fire started. We couldn't hear my mom so when we started to smell smoke we went downstairs, saw my mom lying on the floor, unconscious, and we weren't strong enough to pick her up, so we left her in the house, close to the back door, and called 911."

The officer rubbed his chin in thought. "What was it that you needed to grab, Melanie?"

She had to think of something, "a pad." she said.

Officer Ackerman tilted his head slightly, "a pad?" he asked.

"Yeah, I would have used the ones at Em's house but I have a really heavy flow and the last time I used a pad from Em's house Ibled through."

Officer Ackerman didn't look like he had a clue what Melanie was talking about. He coughed, "Right, next question. What's your mom's full name?"

"Lacie Ivory Adelia," she responded.

"Do you have any idea what could have possibly happened tonight for your mom to pass out, in front of a stove that was on?"

"She's been complaining about her heart recently, it could have been a heart attack."

Officer Ackerman wrote that down as well. He closed his notebook. "That's all the questions I have for you, Melanie. Do you have any other guardian that we can contact when we let you and your friend leave?" He smiled.

She didn't. All of her grandparents were dead, she had no clue where her dad was, and she had no clue if she had any cousins. The closest family that she had outside of her now-dead mom was Emory. "No, the closest person to my family is Emory. I don't have anyone else in my family that I know of."

"That's... unfortunate." He opened his notebook again and wrote what Melanie said down again. 'Do you know your dad's name?"

"No, I haven't seen him since I was, like, seven, at most."

"I guess if your friend's mom is willing to let you stay at their house, we'll tell her to come here when we're ready to let you go." Officer Ackerman stood up and brought Melanie back outside to where Emory was. He then noticed the back-pack that was on the floor in front of Emory. "Miss Brooke, can I see your bag?"

Shit.

Emory looked from the officer then to the bag, to the officer again. "I guess." she trembled as she handed him over the bag.

"Thank you." He took it into the room that they were just in, and a few other officers stepped into the room with him to examine what was in the bag.

Melanie sat down next to Emory, "why do you seem so scared? There can't be anything too bad in your bag right?"

"Did you forget the masks are in that bag?"

Of course they were.

"What?"

"Our masks are in that bag."

Melanie felt like she had just been hit with a sack of bricks. They were in so much shit. What were they going to say if they asked about them? They wouldn't exactly say that they were masks given to them by god that let them kill for him without their identities being revealed. That would get them sent to a mental hospital. Someone had to have seen them walking around the streets with them on, especially with how much time they spent out there trying to find people to kill.

After a few minutes that seemed to drown out into hours, Officer Ackerman came back out and told the girls to come back into the room. There was still the same wooden table, but now there were three chairs on one side (one for each officer), and two on the other (one for Melanie and one for Emory). Officer Ackerman reached into Emory's bag and pulled out both of the masks. "What are these?"

Melanie saw Emory frozen, if that's how she acted around the cops, then there was no way they were going to leave that night. "The masks?" Melanie clarified.

"Yes."

"They're a little inside joke from when we were younger. When we got a little older we made them and we wear them on special days." At least it was a lie that made sense.

Officer Ackerman seemed to take that as an acceptable answer since he put the masks back in the bag. "Melanie, we don't know what's going to happen to your mother."

Where did that come from? She knew that her mother was probably lying dead in a hospital bed right now. "What do you mean?" she asked anyway.

"She suffered some pretty nasty burns. I'm not going to sugarcoat it, she probably won't survive. I'm sorry, kid."

Good. That's what should happen. She couldn't even imagine what Xeno would do if someone they had tried to kill still survived. Melanie looked down, pretending to be sad.

"I guess you girls are good to go now, you've told us everything we need to know." he stood up, walked over to the door, and opened it. He handed Emory her bag on the way out.

Melanie and Emory sat in the police station waiting room, waiting for Emory's mom to pick the two of them up. They watched as multiple officers congregated as the sun kept getting lower and lower. Some of the officers offered Melanie and Emory water, but they refused every time. Emory had said that she once saw that the police could get your DNA from a cup of water you drank from. Whatever, Melanie wasn't that thirsty anyway.

Emory's mom got to the station a couple of minutes after Officer Ackerman called her. When she got there, she rushed in and turned her head around frantically until she found them. When she did, she ran up to them and gave them both a hug. "I'm so happy you guys are okay," she said, as if trying not to cry. "Melanie, it's perfectly okay if you need to stay at our house. Oh, I just hope your mother gets better." Melanie hugged back slightly before Mrs. Brooke pulled away.

On the way to Emory's house, nobody talked. Talking seemed out of place that night.

Once in the house, Emory's mom grabbed some blankets and a pillow and put them on the couch. "Please, get some rest." she said.

Melanie didn't argue. She lay down on the couch under the blankets. It wasn't until then that she noticed how much her clothes smelled like smoke. It wasn't too prominent, but it was there. Melanie shut her eyes and quickly fell asleep.

Chapter 22

She woke up the next morning to the sun blaring in her eyes. She raised her arm to cover her eyes, not ready to wake up.

When she eventually accepted it, she got up and walked around. While walking, she noticed that Emory was also up, walking into the kitchen. "Hey," Melanie said.

"Hey," Emory responded as she got a glass of water from the dispenser in the fridge. "Mom got the news late last night that your mom's officially dead. At least we got the job done."

Melanie laughed slightly. "I guess, but for what? A two-hour police interrogation and now I have to live with... you." she joked.

"Oh haha," Emory said, tilting her head back and forth.

"Did they ever find out what happened through the autopsy?" Melanie asked.

"No," Emory said, "they said that her body was too mangled to find anything."

They were in the clear for another time, and that's all that mattered.

Emory's mom came down the stairs quietly a little bit later. When she got into the kitchen and saw Melanie, her eyes narrowed. "Oh, honey, I'm so sorry," she said as she hugged Melanie.

Melanie hugged back to be nice, even though she couldn't care less about her dead mother. "Oh, it's fine," Melanie said slowly. It seemed to be hurting Emory's mom more than it was hurting her.

Emory's older brother came out of his room, he looked a lot different from the last time that Melanie had seen him, even though she had been at Emory's house a lot. "What the hell is going on?" he asked, rubbing the tiredness away from his eyes.

"Travis, how stupid are you?" Emory scowled.

Emory and Travis looked a lot alike, so much that anybody could mistake them for twins. Travis was three years older than Emory, still lived at home, barely graduated from high school, and never went to college. Both Emory and Travis had brown eyes and brown hair, and they were both tall for their ages. "I'm not slow!" said Travis, "I just don't know what's going on."

"Melanie's mom just died." Emory responded.

"Oh that sucks," he said as he yawned. "Wait, who's Melanie?" he asked.

Nobody responded, so Travis went back into his room.

"I needed to ask, do you want your mom to have a funeral?" Mrs. Brooke asked.

"No," Melanie responded, "she's not a funeral type of person."

"Are you sure?"

"Yes, I'm sure." how couldn't she be sure? She didn't want to have to look at a casket with her dead mom in it, knowing that she caused it. A tomb, maybe. Just to show some respect.

"Okay, but I think we should still put her in a casket and give her a proper burial."

"That's fine by me." Melanie said. Anything to not have to see her mother's face again.

Epilogue

After they had received news that Melanie's mom had been buried at a cemetery, she had thought that she would never want to go. But as months started to pass and the days started to get colder, Melanie felt the urge to go see her tomb at least once.

When she told Emory's parents that she was going out on a walk, they did not question her. Instead of walking around the neighborhood a few times, she took her mask, went outside, and made a portal to where her mom was buried.

She stepped out of the portal and took her mask off, resting it above her head. She looked down at her feet to see a flathead tombstone with her mom's name on it a few feet in front of her. She sat down in front of it silently. She didn't know what to say. After a few minutes of thinking, she started talking. "I'm sorry," she said. "You know I would never do that by choice." her voice broke slightly, and she wiped her right eye. "If you were in the same situation I was in, you would have done what I did too." She sat in silence for a little bit longer, just staring at a plain gravestone with her mom's name, birthday, and death day on it. It's what she would have wanted. She told herself.

"Hey, stranger." Someone called out from a few feet behind her. Melanie quickly hid her mask under her sweatshirt before she turned around. It wasn't until the cold air hit her face that she realized a few tears had rolled down her cheeks, something she never expected.

Behind her stood a girl, with long black hair that reached down to her mid back, piercing blue eyes, and long baggy clothes. She was a few inches taller than Melanie so her head was facing down when she talked to her. "What are you doing out here? It's getting pretty late."

"I could ask you the same thing." Melanie stood up.

"Right right," the girl responded, "so who're you here for?" she asked.

Melanie turned around to look back at her mom's grave. "My mom." She said before looking back. "You?"

The girl sighed, "My grandpa. It's been five years since he passed."

"Sorry about that." Melanie messed with her fingers.

The girl stuck her hand out "Cassidy Brown."

Melanie shook her hand, "Melanie Adelia."

They both stood awkwardly for a while. "Can I get your number?" Cassidy asked.

Melanie quickly stumbled for her phone. "Yeah," she laughed awkwardly.

Why was a random person asking for her number? Why was she giving it to her?

Cassidy typed in her number onto Melanie's phone before smiling "Just send me a text with your name when you get a chance so I can put you in my contacts."

Melanie put her phone away and looked back up at Cassidy. "So do you come here often?" she asked, trying to break whatever type of ice that was there.

"Everybody in my family is buried here, so I do come here pretty frequently. I'd say maybe once or twice a month, you?"

"This is my first time coming here," she pointed to the gravestone behind her, "My Mom died a few months ago, this is the first time I've come here."

"I'm sorry about that." Cassidy frowned, patting Melanie on the shoulder.

Melanie sighed, "Don't be, she was a bitch anyway."

Cassidy pulled her hand away, saying "Alright then." before chuckling. "I should be getting home, it's getting super late. I'll see you around, Melanie." Cassidy turned and began to walk away.

"Oh, yeah, I'll text you later." Melanie felt her face heat up as Cassidy's body began to blend in with the surrounding trees.

"Don't get distracted, she will cause challenges," Xeno said, watching the whole exchange.

"I won't," Melanie replied.

"You better not."